Elza's Kitchen

BY THE SAME AUTHOR

Valeria's Last Stand

Elza's Kitchen

MARC FITTEN

BLOOMSBURY

New York New Delhi London Sydney

First published in Great Britain 2012

Bloomsbury Publishing Plc

50 Bedford Square

London WC1B 3DP

www.bloomsbury.com

Bloomsbury Publishing, London, New Delhi, Berlin and Sydney

A CIP catalogue record for this book is available from the British Library

ISBN 978 1 4088 2132 9

10 9 8 7 6 5 4 3 2 1

Typeset by Westchester Book Group
Printed in Great Britain by Clays ltd, St Ives plc

For Zita

Take all away from me, but leave me Ecstasy,
And I am richer then than all my Fellow Men—
Ill it becometh me to dwell so wealthily
When at my very Door are those possessing more,
In abject poverty—

—Emily Dickinson

Book One

One

Elza awoke alone. Alone and distraught over it. She felt distraught because, quite frankly, though she was not a woman in love, she was a woman who had grown accustomed to company at night; and waking as she had—dressed in scratchy nightclothes and supine in bed—with the bland view of her apartment's ceiling and crown moldings overhead instead of her lover's bristly haunches beside her, and with morning noises from city buses and trams seeping in instead of his heavy breathing in her ear or the smell of food wafting in from her kitchen, for a moment Elza wished to God that she had not woken at all, but rather had slipped mercifully into a heavier slumber—a coma perhaps—or at the very least, into an amorous dream.

While this may have been a distasteful thought to have first thing in the morning, it was no less true. Company at midnight took the edge of a busy day at the restaurant away. A bath after work. A glass of wine. A foot massage she insisted on as foreplay. And then, finally, unapologetic abandonment. Elza required no convincing in this regard, no coaxing, only the foot massage. Her feet massaged and a certain young man. A man she wasn't in love with, but one who was just attentive enough to distract her from her day at work—*their* day at work, really, as they in fact worked together. This special employee possessed the added value of helping her sleep more soundly at night.

But today, this blue-skied Sunday morning, her day off, away from the bustling kitchen of the restaurant, away from her other employees—the dishwasher and the line cooks—well, even on her day off, having missed her evening company, instead of feeling cocksure, she felt irritable. Irritable and unsure . . . confused. Unsatisfied. Untethered. Fitful. Restless. Bitter? Elza considered this. Yes, perhaps even that.

She had reasons to feel bitter, for certain. It happened that Elza had walked Delibab's Centrum alone one recent evening while window-shopping. A photographer had opened a new studio, and in this studio's window hung well-lit and oversized portraits of the traditional middle-class variety: families gathered around their patriarch, done-up wives looking out sunlit windows, children in matching ensembles sitting on rococo chairs, the odd pet. Family scenes being of interest to Elza, particularly because she had none—parents deceased of natural causes, divorced, childless—Elza stopped to look. She examined the portraits for a good five minutes before one of them caught her eye. She gawked open-mouthed. Staring back at her was a photograph of her ex-husband—a man she thought she had loved years ago. He was seated, and a woman and two teenage girls were draped over him. She assumed this was his family. He had daughters! She looked closer. She couldn't decide if the girls were pretty. Actually, best not to bother with them at all. She simply shook her head, looked at her ex-husband, and laughed. The idea of *him* sitting for a portrait seemed fitting. It was the reason they had parted ways all those years ago. He wanted things she didn't. Like sitting for portraits, for starters. Newly wed, he had found a job in the municipal works department in Budapest and a flat in a newly constructed block of buildings. He wanted them to begin a family right away.

"You can cook for *us*," he told her while she was studying at the culinary institute. "For the kids and me."

It was their death sentence. Elza divorced him soon afterward. Eight months into the marriage.

In the photograph in front of her, her ex-husband wore a dark suit. Elza noticed his paunch peeking from his jacket. He looked content. Blissful even. Elza couldn't help but wonder about him. It was twenty years since she had seen him last. It should not have mattered that his picture was here now, in her town. It was only a strange coincidence, care of a transplanted photographer. But still, was she bitter to see this long-lost person happy, to see that he had survived her refusal of him, had thrived, in fact, had succeeded in living his dream, and had even replicated himself? Was she bitter that he had grown into the sort of post-socialist, American-style family man who took portraits of the newly minted bourgeois variety? All toothy wide smiles and plain-spoken earnestness.

She was.

Very.

And the effect of seeing him remained with her long after. An uneasiness followed her around for days and finally settled in her dreams. She awoke regularly—even on blue-skied Sunday mornings like this one—suffering from heartburn and a sour belly, with one hand resting on her stomach. And *this* morning with the other pressed against her forehead. Really pressed against it, as if stuck there, as if to remind her of something important.

Sometime during the middle of the night Elza had awoken with a startled gasp and smacked her forehead with the realization that despite her professional successes, despite her popular restaurant, her material comfort, and her own newly minted bourgeois status, her life was passing her by and she wasn't quite fulfilled. . . .

Two

Fretting was not new to Elza. It was as natural to her as breathing. Witnessing the photograph of her ex-husband was only a trigger. Elza needed challenges in her life, needed to be occupied. Without walls to climb or windmills to attack she was the type of person who became depressed. She knew this. The feeling lived inside her somewhere—probably nestled close to her solar plexus. Yes, it seemed like that was the case. She felt it right in her chest. So, to escape dwelling on her anxieties—which she was prone to do—Elza lived in a state of perpetual movement. If she slowed down or was obstructed, even for a moment, she would suffer being left alone with herself, and then all would be lost.

She pulled her hand away from her head and kicked her thin coverlet aside. She sat at the foot of her bed and reflected on her nighttime memory—which had now metastasized into a larger feeling of regret. She confirmed her feelings were sincere and not her subconscious being melodramatic, the result of having eaten a cold plate of sausage late at night. She tried to remember back to a time when she had felt concretely differently about herself.

Elza arrived at the woeful conclusion that the last time she could remember feeling truly hopeful about life was a staggering twenty years prior—when her skin was a touch more elastic, her hair was uncolored, she was newly freed from a bad marriage, and her future spilled out around her like a tipped-over bag of flour.

She blanched at this realization. Her head began to hurt again. She thought to herself, *How could it all have blown away so quickly?*

A mirror standing in the corner reflected her face: an aging divorcée with crow's-feet at her eyes and lines around her mouth. Years of missteps had taken their toll on her face, she thought. Then came a litany of other faults: She was always a few bills short. She always compromised on the clothing she wore. She was irritatingly soft at the core. Elza caught herself and opened her mouth as if to protest, but no sound escaped. She shook her head at her reflection again. Her skin was sallow and her temples, gray. Her eyes looked sunken in. Her breasts sagged like plastic shopping bags. She tried to force a smile. She pulled her hair back and stuck out her chin. She remembered the younger woman she had been. She thought to herself, *I know I am in there. Somewhere. I know I am still here!*

Elza resolved to coax that hopeful, younger person back into her life. She swept her dark hair onto the crown of her head and hid the graying temples. She took time with her makeup, and when she was done, she really did appear younger, or at least more confident. She looked in the mirror again and forcibly smiled at herself. The distress was still on her mind, but absolutely nothing in her countenance showed it. It was only an ambiguous feeling of dissatisfaction after all.

She decided that a great part of her distress in life came from the fact that so much of it was second rate. Never mind that customers loved her restaurant. Never mind that when they came they usually sought her out as well, to compliment her—especially the men. A potential romance with these men was not a danger. Quite simply, what Elza found dissatisfying was the quality of men who called on her. She was weary of them. She was weary of the lisping Professor of Humanities and his inthethant requeths for Hollandaithe thauthe. Weary of the Postal Inspector, who smiled at her gamely whenever he sloped into the restaurant. Weary, most of all, of the Motorcycle Officer, who never removed his helmet, who sweated profusely at the armpits, and who always placed his sidearm on the table facing toward the other diners, as though he were the protagonist of some forgotten World War Two film. And imagine, *these* were the men worth mentioning! She was equally weary of the rest of them. She wished for a different set of men to want to speak with her. Sophisticated men. Powerful men.

But these second-rate men seemed tethered to her. She knew it was entirely her fault for having encouraged them with smiles and coy banter, for having satisfied their appetites and filled their expanding bellies with her food. But this was the nature of her business. She was a chef, after all; she owned a restaurant. Opening one so soon after socialism's collapse and keeping it going for a decade had required her to be aggressively personable. It was another one of the things her ex-husband had complained about. But in an era of runaway capitalism and millennial madness she knew she had to get along. It was not her fault she understood the need for and perfected the skills of infectious enthusiasm and simulated empathy.

Empathy!

Let us examine here and now the quality of empathy specific to Elza . . .

It was pathological! This is how Elza ran her restaurant. She flooded her customers with aperitifs and sentiment. She buried them in mountains of thick sliced bread and enthusiasm. She was completely at the service of those who mattered. For at least ten years now. Always smiling. Always casting her eyes or fluttering her hands as if she were working a magic show. However, as is life's way, there were hazards, and so the occupational hazard of second-rate men was hers.

Still, none of *this* was necessarily a problem. These were merely the circumstances of her daily life. But today she had awoken with a sense of loss, a fear of her future. A sense that her life had been spent and every second-rate thing she had grabbed hold of thus far would be the end of her tale and the best she could do.

Now, later in the morning, she stood beside her young man—her sous-chef, her employee—in her restaurant's freezer, counting and stocking produce. She wore a tailored pantsuit, a silk blouse with a plunging neckline, a pendant of Venetian glass, and perfect makeup. She had tried to trick herself into feeling better, by looking better. The Sous-Chef said only, "Why are you so dressed up for inventory?"

She tried to turn away from the young man lest he witness her vulnerability. She felt slow and useless in the cold room. She miscounted the eggs in the palette in front of her and began again. *What is the problem?* She could not understand it.

She looked up at the Sous-Chef. She looked at the balanced angles of his face. She watched the muscled cords of his forearms as he lifted large cans onto the shelves above their heads. Her heart should have quickened at the sight of him, but it did not. She felt nothing. The Sous-Chef lowered his eyes and met her gaze. His pupils dilated. He smiled. She did not return it. He leaned in with parted lips.

"Not at work," she snapped, and, turning away, she dropped an egg. The egg cracked open over the others and its yolk slipped. For a second, its yellow yolk kept its shape, but it just as quickly burst open and oozed into a slick mess. It was the third egg she had dropped. Frustrated, one hand fluttered into the air while the other pushed the palette of eggs away.

The young man laughed and grabbed her. He pulled her closer. With his other hand he deftly raised her chin up toward him. He was strong, she thought. Capable. The Sous-Chef kissed her mouth. He kissed her on the neck. It was pleasurable and she thought maybe she should put her arms around him, but she found she could not lift either of them and instead stood awkwardly in the cold room. Her hands remained by her side. Heavy. As though each one were holding a goose by the legs.

"Not at work!" she sighed, between his pecks.

"You're angry with me for something," he said. "I can tell. I can come by tonight, if you like."

He released her face, but kept her body pressed against his own with one arm. He nuzzled and then murmured something in her ear. Even in the freezer, Elza felt her skin glowing. She felt warm. The sheer bulk of him beside her was like standing beside a furnace. She could not decide if any of this made her feel better or worse about herself. It certainly made her feel silly. He released her suddenly without warning. He finished stacking the cans and then left her in the freezer. As he walked past, he sought out her fingers with his own. He winked at her, and Elza shook her head back at him.

"What am I doing?" she whispered to herself when he left.

Weeks passed this way, but Elza managed to keep her growing discomfort from showing. Her growing depression, her despondency, whatever this was, was silent and invisible, as still as a fresh pot of water set to boil. But soon, she began to bubble. She began sleeping later, yet feeling simultaneously as though she had not slept at all. She began arriving at work later than usual. Nobody beyond the Sous-Chef—who often slept beside her—could tell. But even he did not think it serious.

"Of course you're tired," he said understandingly. "Who wouldn't be?"

Elza wanted to scratch him when he said things like that. She didn't want his understanding.

Elza wondered if she was the only person who ever felt this way. Surely, it must be the case, she thought. When she walked through the dining room on the way to the kitchen, or when she was called on, and she looked at her customers, she could not help but think that her customers were wholly unlike her. When she looked into their eyes straining to make some sort of connection, she was surprised by how blissful everybody looked.

The people who dined in her restaurant—Tulip, it was called—*were* satisfied . . . self-satisfied . . . very nearly smug in their satisfaction with life. They saw nothing second-rate about it. To a man, they were no less than fifteen kilograms overweight. To a woman, they were bedazzled and overdone. Fat, newly rich, and mindlessly happy, they were like escaped walruses and ostriches stomping along zoo grounds in top hats and scarves. Existential crisis did not exist in their lives. They ordered lamb; they devoured lamb. Then they licked their lips, picked their teeth, and ordered dessert. They smiled at one another and at their own reflections in the silver mirrors along the walls. They squeezed each other's thighs under the tables. They nodded at one another and belched into their napkins or excused themselves to restrooms where their intestines churned without issue and expelled waste without strain, without sighs, without even a whistle of relief. They returned dreamily to their seats and began again. Like clockwork. As predictable as the Swiss. Life was simple. They needed nothing more than for Elza to smile and nod, encourage them and wind them up from time to time.

Of course, sometimes they had ideas for how she might improve things.

"You should take a table or two away. It would make the dining room less crowded," said one.

"You should put up curtains so we don't have to watch those Gypsies begging outside," said the Professor of Humanities. "They're always about, tapping on the glass, pulling at jackets. They're a nuisance."

"You should make your portions larger."

"You should make your portions smaller."

"I only have your interests at heart!" They all exclaimed this.

Elza opened her eyes wide in response. She thanked them. The corners of her mouth pulled her lips apart in a smile. She grinned for them, two rows of teeth wide. Then she jutted her chin out, pulling the skin underneath taut. She agreed with her customers, no matter what silliness they muttered, and those customers returned her smile. They left large tips for the waitstaff. They returned again and again, for years now. They kept her in business.

Elza had noticed early on, ten years ago, that once released from the clutches of socialism, the masses instantly began twirling like dervishes and shouting with pleasure or for attention, as if they were children let out to recess after years of mental cruelty at the hands of a bitter schoolmarm and her dilapidated classroom.

It was enough, then, for Elza to smile and look into her customers' faces. It was enough for her to nod approvingly and feign interest. Offer a complementary drink or two. Why, with the promise of a full belly and some smiling encouragement Elza realized they could be induced to jump off cliffs en masse! *Yes, yes, we're so very clever. Let's pat ourselves on the back and jump, shall we?*

Elza chuckled. She chuckled at the fact that she could see it so clearly, that she could read her customers so thoroughly, and yet, she never tried to take advantage of them, only sell them Chicken Paprika and Shepherd's Goulash. *How lucky for them*, she thought. Lucky, that she was world-weary and only going through the motions.

But Elza wasn't quite right. It wasn't just her bright smiles that brought people back. It was also the quality of the food. She was a good cook—although Elza didn't cook much herself anymore, spending her time in the dining room or her office—and there was a time when she had cared very much about the food, had paid careful attention to her customers' tastes and desires, to the feedback they gave without knowing it.

She had studied the state her tables were in after her customers were gone. She paid close attention to whether her customers finished their entrées or left stray bites on the plate. She investigated whether desserts had been inhaled or savored. She examined the place settings left behind as though she were a voyeur peering through keyholes into bedrooms at undergarments and shoes, at the shambles of a bed after conjugal visits, at the shambles of a hotel room after a passionate tryst. Elza thoroughly examined her dining area. She took note of how napkins had been left behind. Whether they were placed carefully beside a plate or thrown over it. Whether they were forgotten on the floor. Whether they were stained. And if so, how stained were they? Blotches of sauce? Cream stains? Coffee splatters? These things mattered. She did not give a damn about what her customers said because they left truer evidence behind on the sheets, and Elza divined future sales from her napkins. Indeed, it was in the frantic manner of their twisted napkins that she had learned what dishes to make more of, what desserts to make less, what to have on stock and ready to go, and what should be made only when needed.

Quality and care had built the restaurant. And it had produced very good food.

Take, for instance, her Chicken Paprika. Except for her Shepherd's Goulash, there wasn't a more quotidian meal in Hungary. There wasn't a more basic dish on the menu. It was a staple after all. Previously a meal for healthy, growing proletariat families. For how many decades, mothers and grandmothers had whipped it together in minutes and fed it to their hungry children, and generally, the hardest part about it was killing the chicken or not burning the paprika. Otherwise, it was an easy meal to prepare. Elza's ingredients—the breast of a young and plump chicken from the countryside, the reddest paprika she could find, purple onions, salt, silky sour cream, and freshly milled flour—were readily available. She enjoyed cooking fresh and teasing out the flavor of the food, of the entire country. In fact, every forkful eaten was a matter of national pride.

Her Chicken Paprika was tangy with the slightest hint of sweetness to it. Elza served it over a bed of egg noodles, and it was simple country food, a kitchen classic. At one thousand forints a plate it was also her strongest-selling entrée, exactly the same as and wholly unlike any Chicken Paprika any of her customers had ever tasted.

"Reminds me of my grandmother," a customer might exclaim after the first hot bite.

Others would nod, savor what was in their mouths, and point at their plates. They watched the steam curl up in tendrils and carry the aroma to their noses. They thought of country kitchens on the plains, of short pants, and of being chased by geese.

"This is better than my grandmother's," another customer would venture.

"Better?" the Motorcycle Officer mused. He loved his grandmother. Admitting something like this felt like a betrayal. He wiped his brow with a napkin. He spun his revolver around on the table.

"Sweeter," he offered. "No, tangier."

"Sweeter? Tangier? Yes. Yes. All of that," said another man.

They ate silently. They focused and began the pleasant task of shoveling heaping forkfuls of chicken and noodles into their mouths. They sighed. Their eyes welled with tears as they remembered their doting grandmothers.

The savory sauce ran down their throats. The pasta melted over their tongues. They chewed their succulent chicken, and it yielded to the heat inside their mouths. They swallowed and wanted to giggle. Over poultry! No other words passed between them while they ate. Their arms and hands moved quickly over their plates. They mopped up the deep pink sauce and flecks of meat with their bread, practically moaning in pleasure meanwhile. When they finished eating, they beckoned for the waiter. He approached them confidently and nodded, never mind that he was young and his bow tie was askew. They asked him what was in the Chicken Paprika. Always the same question. Every time they ordered it. What extra ingredient was carrying them so dangerously close to delicious convulsions?

"It's chicken," the waiter stated flatly, then looked off into space.

The diners shook their heads. They pointed at their polished plates and flushed cheeks.

"No, no, no. My daft young man, I know it's chicken! I can see that it's chicken! There's more here. There's more. I can taste it. I want to know what it is. What is it?"

The waiter offered a half-smile but continued to stare into space. The customers balked.

"Please ask the chef to come out," they requested.

And Elza was summoned from her office in the kitchen where she had been spinning pencils and reading a magazine while the Sous-Chef and the rest of her cooks made the meals she had taught them all how to prepare. She presented herself to her customers. She smiled. She looked at the flushed skin. She looked at their hands still violently twisting her cloth napkins. Postcoital. She jutted her chin out and smiled.

"What is in this?" they asked her straightaway.

"It's Chicken Paprika," she said.

"But what's in it? This sauce?"

"Ah," she smiled. "It's only what you would expect. A few onions, some paprika."

"Yes, but what is in the sauce?"

Elza smiled wider. She looked at the waiter and rested her fluttering hands on his shoulder. "I'm afraid we can't say. It's our secret recipe. You'll just have to come again."

Her diners begged, but it was useless. Instead, she offered them a choice of port or Tokaj, which the waiter poured. The sweetness shut them up. She watched their eyes close as they swallowed. It was like one final tug of their sex. One final flick of the tongue. They were speechless. In awe and reverent. Thankful. Ecstatic. Elza only walked away, wishing something or someone could stroke her into such euphoria.

And herein begins her very specific troubles: after she recognized it one blue-skied Sunday morning, Elza's quiet dissatisfaction with life began to grow, and as it did, she began tossing every night—the Sous-Chef beside her or not. She began grinding her teeth and mumbling in her sleep. Her head pulsed with every heartbeat. She kicked her sheets off while she slept. When he was sleeping beside her, she kicked the Sous-Chef in the shins with jerky movements that seemed like running, as though she were running away in her dreams, as though she could not run away quickly enough. Some nights the young man would wake with a curse after she had kicked him.

"What's the matter?" he asked. He sat up and looked around, and his eyes rested on Elza's hip and bottom. He would smile at her and caress the back of her naked shoulders, and despite the fact that she knew he was part of the problem, that he was also an employee, and far too young for her, Elza felt she needed some kind of intimacy, and she could not help herself, so she began sharing everything that was on her mind. She would pull his arm around her shoulder, take his hand in hers, hold it against her breast, and with her back to him, she spilled her heart out with a level of intensity that always surprised them both, with a gravity that, in his youth or perhaps only maleness, he found disconcerting and mysterious, incomprehensible. She didn't care. It was a conundrum. But what else could she do?

"What else can I do?" she asked the Sous-Chef one night when she was particularly down. She did not know what she was thinking opening up to him this way. She knew their relationship was a part of her problem.

"You have everything!" he said and motioned around her flat, at the art on her walls, the television, the polished floors, the furniture, and her dressers full of clothing and jewelry. "You're rich! You should learn to enjoy it more."

"I'm not rich," she answered. She looked around and waved her hands. It all looked worthless to her.

"You have a nice flat, your own restaurant, and you vacation in Corfu nearly every summer. I'm sorry, but I can't feel sorry for you."

"I'm still paying for it all," she said. "I have to work."

The Sous-Chef shook his head and embraced her. He kissed her forehead. "Then you're just a whiny, miserable capitalist," he said, "and you'll never have enough. I share a flat with my mother and sister. I *have* to work . . . but I wouldn't call myself poor either."

She sighed.

He sighed.

The Sous-Chef could have told her that she was as much a spinning child as the rest of her countrymen, one who wanted things her way but didn't quite know what she wanted. But he would not dare. She was *his* employer, after all, and as he had mentioned, he needed to work. But in shops or restaurants, on the tram, or at the train station, he watched as she threw her advice and forints around as easily as if they were confetti. The Sous-Chef knew, had experienced, that Elza had an opinion about everything. Though she did not drive, did not do her own laundry, or sweep, the Sous-Chef had witnessed her explain to others the best way to change a tire, the best way to remove a stain from a pair of pants, the best way to sweep a sidewalk, and, most importantly, the best way to prepare a partridge. When he made a suggestion about the kitchen that he felt would make it more efficient, more often than not, Elza shut him down with an indulgent smile and a pinch on the cheek.

"I went to culinary school as well, you know?" he would mutter.

She was really a difficult woman, he thought. The Sous-Chef thought she needed something to keep her from being so self-absorbed. He thought she needed a family.

None of this made the Sous-Chef care for Elza any less. He cared a great deal about her. And he really couldn't think of what to do for her save flash a smile, and maybe, if she didn't turn her face away, maybe brush her long dark bangs out of her eyes and hold her by the back of her head before kissing her slender neck.

Elza told him how lonely she felt. How despondent she was. How empty her work seemed and how she wanted desperately to connect with something bigger than what she had connected with so far in her forty-eight years. She told him that she couldn't understand how that could be. She told him about a photograph of her ex-husband she had found. She told him that she was having a crisis and could not understand where the feeling was coming from. She knew she was successful, and that she had a nice flat and nice things, but those things seemed disassociated from her life. Unreal, even. Outside of her. Her life itself just never seemed big enough or sweet enough. There was no better explanation than that. She wanted more, and she was at a loss in explaining why.

"Oh," the Sous-Chef said good-naturedly when she had finished speaking. He pulled his hand free from hers and traced her shoulder with a fingertip. He pulled her curtain of dark hair aside and kissed a mole on the back of her neck. "You're still thinking about all that? I thought maybe a spider bit you. I've killed a lot of them around here lately. Have you noticed? Would you like me to bring you a glass of water?"

Elza was deflated. She understood that it was not the younger man's fault that he was a younger man, but her understanding did not make her feel any less silly for having exposed herself to him. She thought about those older men from the restaurant at these moments. She wondered if the Professor of Humanities would be more communicative or if the Motorcycle Officer would make her feel safe. She wondered if those older men would simply be more set in their ways. She decided that while an older man might have understood, he would also have been incapable of the passion and vigor and brief respites her young sous-chef brought to her bedroom at night. She sighed and turned toward the Sous-Chef. She looked at him. There was his charm! No denying it. He was fit and handsome. His arms were solid. His teeth were straight and white.

She thought about how precious he looked sleeping beside her, like a darling angel, a cherub on a cake. She touched the hairs of his chest and felt a pang of conscience. She did not really care about him. And her hand looked old against him.

And as if to torture her . . .

"You should marry me," he whispered.

Lately, he had taken to proposing, as though her problem were something he could fix with the promise of marriage. She laughed at him and told him he was crazy. She was eighteen years older. The notion of marrying him was ridiculous. Besides, beautiful as he was, Elza did not love him and could not bring herself to tell him that. She was fond of him, certainly. He was young and silly and handsome and fun, and all of that was nice and charming, but to marry him . . .

"Think about it," he argued. "We could have children! It's not too late. There's still time. Just a little bit, but it's possible."

Elza scoffed. "No, no, how would that look?"

"Who cares?" the young man muttered, and Elza could see that he was becoming more frustrated by her refusals, that he was growing tired of her rejections. "We've been doing this for three years now," he said. "I'm thirty. I'm old enough to be married. I love you. I want a family. You need a family."

Elza did not answer him. She never did. Instead, she turned away again. She presented her naked back to him and pretended to fall asleep. The Sous-Chef sighed and lowered his head to his pillow. She listened to his shallow breathing. She felt his body tense behind her. His bristly parts were pulled away from her. She knew it was only a matter of time before he left her. She did not expect she would mind at all.

Three

For weeks, Elza carried her feelings around as though she were carrying a pot of steaming soup through a crowded room. This pot was filled to the brim, and unwieldy, and Elza felt herself barely capable of keeping the sloshing contents from pouring over her guests or herself. She felt as if anything might set her to stumbling—an unkind word, a cross look—and she was not sure what her response might be. She was in a state in which she could see herself dissolving into tears or bursting out in fury.

However, she could also not help but think she was carrying the answer to her own crisis inside that pot. A dumpling of hope sunk deep in the Pandora's mix, as it were. She knew the only way to get to it would be to let the pot go. But the mess, she thought. The stinking mess.

Perhaps, she decided instead, perhaps if she could slow her thinking down enough, if she could become lost in a simple function like walking, she might build an appetite and eventually drink down the mess. There had to be an answer to her questions.

So, after lunch services were finished, she set out exploring the city and the topography of her soul. Her sous-chef followed her out the door and asked if she needed company, but Elza shook her head. She was sure he couldn't help her. She told him to get to know the new pastry chef instead, a young graduate from the culinary institute—a young woman named Dora who had started in the kitchen and who had seemed talented from the start.

"Are you all right?" the Sous-Chef asked. He had noticed that her face was looking haggard recently, but he didn't say anything about it. "You came in very late today. Lunch was nearly over."

"I'm fine," she said. "You've got it under control anyway. You don't need me."

The Sous-Chef tried to peck her on the cheek, but as they were standing in front of the restaurant, Elza would not let him. Before he could connect, she stepped aside and began walking away briskly.

"Where are you going?" the Sous-Chef asked. "You live that way."

"May I walk where I like?" Elza snapped at him and immediately felt sorry. He was only trying to be helpful. He was not unlike a retriever in that regard. He stood in front of the restaurant with a tilted head and a perplexed look on his face, as if she'd kicked him without cause. "You can meet me at the flat later," she offered.

She waved good-bye and continued on in the opposite direction of her flat and away from the Centrum. She wanted to explore pockets of the city that she hadn't before, and it was a large enough city that there were always places for her to rediscover, to get to know more intimately. There were always parts of the city of Delibab for her to lose herself in.

She began at the church, on the grounds that the city was arranged in a manner by which the church stood proudly at the center, and everything else radiated from that point.

She walked aimlessly at first, up the promenade toward the train station, past the shops and boutiques that hawked and hawked, endlessly hawking now. Everything from scarves to sunglasses, from exotic vacations to fast food—so different from the old days, it bombarded her—and Elza walked aimlessly around this plenty wondering how it all managed to keep standing, wondering who was buying it all. She felt herself shrinking in it. Every placard in every mobile phone store, in every grocery store, in every boutique, and in every department store had smiling faces on them. None of them matched her mood. She walked past the new shopping mall. She remembered walking into the mall when it was finally completed and standing wide-eyed like everyone else. She remembered that she'd walked on the tiled floors, ordered an ice-cream cone at the food court, window-shopped, and finally gone to a movie. When she had left it was dark outside and she had wondered how a day could have passed so uneventfully. She had not returned to the mall.

She turned off of the promenade about halfway to the train station. She turned down a street and decided to walk away, to walk out toward those pockets of the city where development had not arrived, where development might never arrive. Those places still existed outside of the Centrum. Out on the outskirts of Delibab, or out near the Great Forest and Park where a few cottages and villas stood. There were also the pockets of concrete block-housing that had gone up during socialism—cities unto themselves. Elza walked there. A different kind of life flourished in these places. One she recognized from childhood. The domestic life. A human chorus that had existed long before she ever had. A chorus that washed over her had reminded her of the past. It was the sound of children's voices here; the scratch of a broom against concrete there. Faint strains of music playing through open windows. *Life!* Connected in intricate and myriad ways. Attachments of all sorts. All the things Elza recognized she was missing. This sort of living seemed real in a different way. Being able to witness it comforted her. At last, she found herself in the Roma quarter. She knew where she was because she spotted the flower girl who visited her restaurant at night selling wild roses. The district was beaten up. It was not glimmering or polished like her street in the Centrum. Garish lights in front of neighborhood taverns, roofs missing shingles, red lamps glowing in front of nondescript buildings. Fallen plaster everywhere. It was the sort of district that was understood to be unwise to walk through at night.

The flower girl was walking purposefully and Elza, having never really considered this girl's life outside of the restaurant before, followed her from a distance, curious to see how she lived, where she went. When the girl disappeared behind a tall fence, Elza hurried to where she had entered and peeked between slats of wood. *So this is where the flower girl lives!* She saw a courtyard that was unkempt, with building materials and kitchen litter strewn about. Some boys came out of the house and into the courtyard. Elza recognized them, too. They were always hanging around the restaurant, but not with anything to sell. She was surprised to see them, surprised to discover that there was some kind of relation between them all. She had never given any deeper thoughts to these people, although she saw them nearly every day. Suddenly, she was afraid they would catch her spying on them. How would she have explained that? Anyway, she'd walked enough for the day, so she turned and headed back to the Centrum. She would go home and rest before dinner service began.

Elza's flat was on the fourth floor of a neo-baroque building that overlooked the promenade in the Centrum. When people commented on her fortune, she shrugged.

"It's not Budapest," she said. "It's only Delibab."

The Sous-Chef was waiting at her door when she walked up. Remembering how she had snapped at him and feeling bad about it, she smiled as she approached. She held the door open for him.

"Feeling better?" he asked with genuine concern.

"A bit," she said, and she followed him inside.

Entering her apartment after the long walk, Elza saw anew her sitting room and the freshly painted French doors that opened onto the small balcony over the boulevard. She considered the unhindered views of the church at the city's center. *Maybe I am rich*, she thought. *But how did that happen?*

Early evening arrived, and the sun dropped and cast a gloaming light across the boulevard. The Sous-Chef was napping. Elza sat on her balcony, watching the trams go past. Her eyes wandered to the church spires. At this particular moment, the clocks were nearing six. People were hurrying home. *Always hurrying now*, she thought. The world had been simpler when she was a child. The country had been simpler. Not nearly as much unnecessary movement as there seemed to be today. Elza's ennui had quieted for the moment. It seemed walks were a good idea. She sat for a bit to think about the restaurant. She ran the menu over in her mind.

As the restaurant was her main concern in life, she decided that maybe something there needed changing. Maybe she needed to challenge herself. She thought a little about it. Maybe Tulip could stand an addition to the menu, or maybe a new menu entirely. Things were becoming staid. Perhaps this was the extent of her troubles. Maybe she should work at acquiring some recognition in the restaurant world. She should use her imagination more. She could do anything she wanted. She could create new meals. *I could get a star! A Michelin star! Why not? Or maybe a review? A serious review written by a serious critic!* A few challenges, a stated purpose—that might be all she needed to get herself out of her funk.

Suppertime was approaching, and cooking smells began wafting into her flat from the other flats in her building. She cataloged them in her mind. There was the hint of crushed garlic. There was vegetable oil. There was the ubiquitous paprika.

She would have let herself surrender to the bouquet of aromas, but she could not because the church bells began to chime and jarred her concentration. Six o'clock meant opening the restaurant for dinner service. Her young sous-chef stirred in the bedroom behind her.

He stumbled out and she watched him scratch himself sleepily. He looked like a child and she shook her head. Maybe she was fond of him in the day, she relented; she was certain she was sort of fond of him at twilight, but all of that dissipated once the sun had set and he was her employee again.

The Sous-Chef headed to the shower. He left her apartment before she did when they spent time together like this. He was the one who opened the restaurant for dinner service and met the other employees.

"Someone is using dill," she called out to him a few minutes later when he had finished bathing.

The young man came to her side and dressed quickly into his kitchen whites. He inhaled and nodded.

"You're right," he said. "Maybe they're pickling something."

"I smell paprika, also," she said. "I was imagining a paprika and dill sauce. Good idea, don't you think? Maybe we could add something like it to the menu? A new signature dish. A pork knuckle? Rabbit?"

The Sous-Chef grunted. His senses were as active as hers, but he liked to think he was not as sentimental about things as she was. He was strictly a businessman, he liked to say. He wanted a new flat and his own restaurant, and he was unapologetic about it. One day soon, he often told himself. He sniffed the air a second time. "They're using too much dill, whatever they're doing. But your sauce might taste good on a pork tenderloin," he said. "Roasted, maybe?"

"Oh! Good idea," she said. "A pork tenderloin in a paprika dill sauce. Marinated in white wine."

He shook his head and made a face. "Brined pork loin. And we could use the potato dumplings as a side. They're cheap and everybody loves them anyway."

She smiled. There it was! She recognized a glimpse of it. Contentment. So easy. Maybe if she did more of the cooking herself. She was content when she worked in the kitchen. She imagined the pork tenderloin marinated in white wine, in a paprika dill sauce, with moist dumplings on the side, and a dry white wine for the palate. She ran the presentation over in her head. A cucumber salad alongside. Some garnish on the side of the roasted meat—parsley, perhaps. A dramatic presentation. They could serve the dish in one of the larger plates they used for game hens. The sauce could be drizzled over the top.

As always, a list of ingredients crossed her mind: fresh dill, red onions, crushed garlic, paprika, and lean pork tenderloin, all the fat cut away, maybe cubed and saved for flavor somewhere else. It sounded good. She thought about her restaurant's star. She thought about a review.

The Sous-Chef kissed her forehead and hurried out.

"I love that head of yours," he said. "Stay and think; I've got to get to the restaurant."

She was left sitting on her balcony alone.

Elza looked out at the doleful hotel directly across the street.

Somehow it had missed out on the city's beautification. The Austrian owners had only recently started to replace the sagging awnings. She could see they were trying to put in air-conditioning now. She looked at its facade and at the street in front. She spotted the Sous Chef and waved down to him when she saw him crossing. He looked up and smiled. He blew her a kiss. He turned around and ran across the road. He darted between two trams and was soon heading toward Tulip, which was on the very next street, parallel to the promenade, behind the hotel.

Elza stood and closed the French doors. She shut out the street noise. She imagined the Sous-Chef arriving at the restaurant. She imagined him entering the dining room, decorated to look like a roadside inn from an older era. There were large picture windows at the front and thirty-five candlelit tables. There were concave silver mirrors on the wall and high-backed chairs with arm rests. She had regular customers from the neighborhood—a healthy lunch business, a robust dinner service. Around one corner from the restaurant was the Russian consulate, and around the other was the refurbished synagogue. People came from both for her potato pancakes—golden fried disks covered with a healthy dollop of sour cream and shredded Havarti cheese. The sour cream had minced garlic in it that made mouths water.

And now she realized that, following a direct line, the Roma quarter where she had been walking was not too much farther. Roma children came tearing down the street at all hours passing the restaurant as they headed toward the Centrum. Sometimes they would stop and peer inside the restaurant through the picture windows. They tapped on the panes of glass, made faces at the customers, or begged for money before Elza or one of her employees shooed them away. Elza thought about them now. All in all she did not mind them. She thought they added something to the ambience of the place. There were, of course, times when they were a bit too rambunctious for her taste, when they rapped against the glass a bit too hard and frightened people into thinking it might break, or sometimes they accosted customers heading out a bit too aggressively. There were times when they pulled coattails too roughly, wouldn't let go of wrists, tried to steal watches. Elza had to leave the kitchen and speak sternly with them when they acted like that. They generally listened and scurried off, but sometimes they ignored her and kept right on pulling. One could never tell what they would do. They appeared and left like summer storms. She did not mind them, though. She often slipped them loose change or Linzer cookies when she had extra.

Elza left the balcony and went inside. She picked up a foreign magazine from her sofa. It was her favorite restaurant magazine: *Le Gourmand*. She thumbed the pages. Thinking of her restaurant fondly from a distance, she thought others might appreciate it, too. A critic might. The magazine opened to a well-worn page, to a photograph of a man, his monthly column underneath. He was her favorite. *Why not start with him?* she thought to herself. *I should get him here. He would love this place. I am sure this man would love my restaurant . . .*

And at precisely that moment, she decided that somehow, one way or another, she would get this critic—she looked at his picture and unpronounceable Italian name—to visit Tulip. He would write a review of her restaurant. A glowing review! *Le Gourmand* sponsored an annual prize, the Silver Ladle; she should try and get Tulip nominated.

She looked at the photograph of him seated at a table as she had probably a hundred times that month, as she did a hundred times every month. She bought the magazine specifically because she liked looking at him sitting in different dining rooms across Europe. She could only barely read his column—she'd studied French in high school, and knew most of the food words from culinary school—but Elza could tell by his napkin and by his spent place settings whether he had enjoyed his meals or not.

In this picture, she could see that the paunchy man behind glasses and a thick beard was unsatisfied. His jowls were pulled in firmly. His eyes were ruddy. She looked at his napkin and by the stains on it divined that he had not liked the meal he had just eaten. She also divined that he would love her pork tenderloin. *This is a fabulous idea*, she told herself, excited now, *but how can I reach him?*

She dressed as quickly as she could, hurried to her office, and began calling colleagues and restaurateurs she knew around Budapest. She would convince the critic to come, and she would create for his visit a new signature meal. While on the telephone, she rifled through the refrigerator to find a pork loin. The kitchen brigade watched her quizzically as she ran back and forth from her office to the pantry and the refrigerator. When she found the loin she wanted she marched it out and held it up.

"I need this," she called out to her employees. "Nobody touch it."

"What are you doing? You're fluttering all over the kitchen," said the Sous-Chef when he was able to get her attention. "Are you really thinking of that pork dish? I can do it, if you want. Why don't you go back to your office?"

Elza shook her head. "I'm making this," she said. "I'll handle it."

The Sous-Chef nodded and made space for her near his station.

She began by preparing a marinade. She decided on a simple white-wine mixture that included parsley, garlic, salt, and black pepper. She mixed the ingredients and bathed the loin in a covered dish, which she put back into the refrigerator. Then she went to her office to try a few more calls. They were all fruitless. Only a few of her colleagues had any idea what she was asking them.

"I don't read those magazines," said one chef. "They're only interested in French cuisine."

Those chefs who *did* read the magazine thought it was an impossible idea.

"I don't think it works like that. You can't request a specific critic for your restaurant. It's impossible."

The next morning she started her day by making international calls from home. She called the offices on the magazine's masthead. They spoke French there. Elza tried a few halting words, but they hung up. Later, she researched and called restaurants the critic had visited. Nobody had information about him or how to reach him.

"Anyway, he was not friendly," a chef in Vienna warned her. "I got a good review, but he was not friendly."

Elza thanked him while looking at the corresponding photograph of the critic's visit. She saw that the Italian looked contented. She congratulated the restaurant owner on the positive review.

After a few more fruitless calls, she thought about the pork loin in the refrigerator and decided she'd be better off working on the meal anyway. She went to the restaurant well before lunch service so she could have the kitchen to herself. She went about gathering the ingredients she'd come up with the previous night, everything from sifted flour, to sour cream, to fresh sprigs of dill, to a mildly spicy paprika, to minced garlic, a pair of medium onions, butter, and olive oil.

She sliced off two generous portions of the marinated loin and dredged them in flour. She chopped the onions, heated the butter and olive oil in a large skillet, and, when the fats began to hiss and spit at her, she smiled and dropped in the chopped onions and then the pork loin. The food hissed in the pan, and the smell of onion and garlic hit her nose immediately. Her stomach growled. She browned the meat on both sides and cooked everything until the onions were caramelized. When they had reduced to a fraction of their original size and the meat was sufficiently brown, she added the paprika. She stirred it into the mixture of onions and butter and olive oil. She stirred it around the skillet, over the pork loin. She lifted the skillet off of the flame to keep the paprika from burning. She lifted it and stirred, until everything was a deep and rich red—the color of an apple skin. She lowered the heat and let the skillet cool a bit before returning it to the flame. She covered it and let it stew.

In a ceramic bowl she mixed sour cream, a bit of flour, and fresh dill. This was the key to the meal. This was her sauce. She stirred until it was all smooth. She had thirty minutes in front of her, before she could add it, so she took the time to make her phone call. She asked a receptionist after two instructors she had been fond of. She was given a telephone number, but before she called it she went back to the kitchen and removed the lid to the skillet and slowly spooned the sauce in. The onions and paprika blended with the cream and dill. She stirred slowly, a spoonful at a time, and everything took on the color of salmon. She tasted a bit and nodded. The dill was pungent. The paprika was tangy. The texture was creamy. Elza's mouth watered and she wanted to dig into the rest of it right away. She didn't. She turned off the stove and moved the pan from the range. She left it covered. She went back to the refrigerator and found a few prepared dumplings. She warmed them in another skillet under a low heat. She opened a bottle of white wine. She made herself an actual plate. She garnished it with parsley. She carried the entrée out to the dining room and arranged it on the table.

She stood over it and looked. She lit a candle. She sat down to eat.

When that first bite passed her lips and fell on her tongue, she couldn't help but sigh. The sauce was good. It exploded in her mouth. It was spicy and creamy and rich and filling. She cut through the meat and took a sliver in her mouth. Perfectly tender meat! Hints of the wine spread across her mouth and into the back of the throat. She chewed and swallowed and ate her meal. She drank her glass of white wine. She enjoyed it! She really enjoyed it! She was excited by the meal. Simple, tasteful, perfect.

She finished just as the Sous-Chef arrived to open for lunch preparations. He was surprised to find her sitting in the dining room.

"What are you doing here so early?" he asked.

"There's some food left in the kitchen." She pointed at her plate. "Try it!"

She followed him into the kitchen where he made a beeline for the stove. He didn't bother to dish it out the way she had. He lifted the lid, nodded appreciatively, and dug in. He took a bite.

"The sauce is great," he said. He cut a bite of meat and chewed. "The meat is tender! What is that taste? Is that white wine? I told you to brine it."

Elza's face fell. "You don't like it?"

"No, I'm not saying that. It's great. I just prefer pork that's been brined. Just my taste."

Elza shook her head.

"I prefer the white wine. The marinade. It's more subtle."

The Sous-Chef shook his head. "A simple brine. I'll make another one later and show you how I mean. You'll see."

They looked at each other and Elza shrugged. She took the skillet away from him before he could take another bite and prepared herself a second plate. She retreated to her office to make more calls.

"I just think it's better to brine pork," he called after her. "I don't see why you have to get crabby."

Elza closed her office door.

She reached a former classmate who suggested she contact their old culinary school. She remembered the pair of professors, worldly sorts who might be able to help. She called the school, but they had both retired. The office had the same phone number listed for the both of them. Elza was surprised to learn that the two men lived together in Budapest. They were delighted to hear from her, they said, and Elza smiled at being so fondly remembered; they each picked up a telephone, and when they heard about how well she had done over the last decade, they congratulated her and told her how happy they were. The first instructor had been professor of sauces; the other had been professor of meats.

"Your success is no surprise. You were one of my most talented students," said the Professor of Sauces.

"I knew you would do well," said the Professor of Meats.

She thanked them and invited them to Delibab for a special dinner. She told them she had a new meal she wanted them to try right away. They agreed to come for the weekend.

When they arrived on Saturday, she gave them a tour of the kitchen and introduced them to her sous-chef. Having argued for a week over his suggestion of brining the pork, the Sous-Chef was in a foul mood. In truth, it wasn't just the pork. What he was really angry about was Elza's latest refusal to another marriage proposal.

"This isn't going to work for me anymore," he had said in bed the Saturday before.

"We will only marinate with the white wine," she had answered. "I think brining will spoil the flavor. The brine will overpower everything else. And it's just too . . . common."

"You're not going to answer? Elza, don't you want to marry me?" the Sous-Chef had countered. "And brine won't spoil anything. Pork is always brined. It's not *common*; it's just the way it's done."

"It's my recipe and my restaurant!" Elza had said and was sorry she had. The Sous-Chef had got out of bed and dressed.

"If you don't want brined pork, you don't want it," he had said. "Fine. I'll do it your way . . . for now. But this isn't working for me, Elza. You have to understand that."

He had left and taken with him as many of his things as he could carry. He hadn't returned all week. He had met her at work and fumed in the kitchen. He had banged pots and shouted at the line cooks. He had smiled only at the new pastry chef.

However, Elza knew she could count on him, and when she and her former instructors took seats in the dining room and the waiter presented them with their meals, she was happy to see that her sous-chef had prepared the entrée exactly as the recipe instructed.

The two instructors breathed in the scent of the marinated meat and sauce. The aroma of dill made the sides of their tongues water. They nodded appreciatively at the presentation and slowly dissected the tenderloin. It was roasted, blackened in places, but was tender and moist. When they took their knives to the pork and carved a bite, they could see how juicy the meat was—juicy and tender! It could have been a piece of fruit, it was so tender. The professors moved in unison. They carved and ate as if it had been choreographed. They savored their bites, but did so with efficient quick chews. They nodded at her as the juice and the sauce spread over their tongues and down into their stomachs. Elza wore her whitest kitchen uniform, as if she were back taking exams. When the two men finished their meals, finished their wine, before they said anything, she poured them each a glass of Tokaj and asked the waiter to bring in some freshly made cottage-cheese cake topped in red currant sauce. They drank and then dipped their spoons in the rich cream. Their eyes were heavy.

"How was it?" she asked.

"Mmm," sputtered the Professor of Sauces. "Elza, this meal was exquisite. The sauce is divine."

"Yes, yes," said the Professor of Meats and nodded. "Delicious. You've done something fabulous. The meat was prepared perfectly. It was tender and juicy. I agree that the sauce was fantastic. A subtle hint of wine. Excellent."

The first instructor nodded. "And this cottage-cheese cake! This is your pastry chef's doing, yes? It's wonderful that you hired someone from the same institute."

Elza smiled and produced the magazine. It was time to get down to business. She opened it to the Critic's column. She pointed at him.

"Do you know this man?" she asked them. "Do you know the prize the magazine gives? The Silver Ladle? I want him to visit us here. I want him to review the restaurant. I want to win the Ladle."

The Professor of Sauces whistled when he saw the photograph. The other scoffed.

"I know of him by reputation," the Professor of Sauces said while shaking his head. "Only that way."

"He's a fraud," said the Professor of Meats.

"He's not," countered the Professor of Sauces. "He's a demagogue with a refined palate!"

"Bah! He's a ruffian! A fraud!"

"He destroyed Les Demoiselles d'Avignon."

"But he's a fraud!"

"They lost their Michelin star. A fraudster could not cause that kind of damage."

Elza considered the photograph. The story of the French restaurant in Barcelona had become legend. Les Demoiselles d'Avignon had been in business for six years. The chef de cuisine was a Frenchman from an old culinary family. After he had studied and then apprenticed at the best restaurants in Paris—his family's—he had left for Barcelona to expand the business into Spain.

"I did not know this man was that same critic," Elza said. She looked at the Critic's picture with concern.

"Yes, yes, the very same," the Professor of Meats explained. "He wrote that their foie gras tasted like old chicken livers, or was it tuna fish? Either way, he said it was only fit for a dying cat."

"He said this?" Elza asked.

The two men nodded.

"Was it true?" she asked.

The two men shrugged.

"Who knows? But the restaurant suffered a devastating blow after that," the Professor of Meats continued. He pointed at the photograph. "What was especially cruel was that he dared to return after the review was printed. He ordered the same meal. He ate everything on the plate a second time and then he shook his head. When the young chef heard the Critic was there, he took off his hat and chased the Italian out of the restaurant and down the street with a carving knife. Said he wouldn't know foie gras from his mother's tit. It took the entire kitchen staff to keep him from killing the man. They chased their employer down the street. Maître d', pastry chef, bathroom attendant. It took all of them to pull him off. And he was cursing at the Critic all the while. Horrible Catalan curses he had learned in the fish markets. With his employees holding the chef back, the Critic stood up and dusted his pants. He made some kind of Italian gesture at the chef. Then he turned and walked away. He published a second article! It was an unprecedented thing, and the review was even more scathing than the first. And all of this before the Michelin guide was going to press. They investigated the matter. While they did, of course they removed a star. They printed the guide with the missing star and a notation that a review was pending. The chef's family was embarrassed, of course. The young chef, not willing to accept it, unable to fight it, sealed himself in his restaurant's kitchen, turned on the gas, and stuck his head in the oven."

"Tsk, tsk, tsk," the Professor of Meats said. "A ruffian!"

"It was a pity," said the Professor of Sauces while nodding. "The editorial board determined that the chef's fois gras had indeed been made from goose! They were coming from his family's farm in Brittany."

Elza considered the information. She looked at the wiry hair on the Italian's face. She thought about the Silver Ladle and shrugged her fear away.

"How could he get away with this?" she asked.

"Well, he defended himself by saying that he had written that the foie gras had 'tasted' like tuna fish. Not his fault the young man overreacted."

Elza put the magazine down but kept her eyes on the Critic's face and his napkin. *This is a peasant*, she decided. *This is not the kind of man who eats fois gras and snails. This is the kind of man who eats roasted pig. Who probably grew up eating tripe*. Elza thought he would like her pork tenderloin. In fact, she knew he would.

She lost herself in the picture a moment longer. She was about to ask them—she didn't know why—if they knew whether the Critic was married when there was a sudden rapping against the window next to them. They all looked up. Elza waved the children away with her hand. She shook her head at them.

"I'm sorry. Ignore them," she apologized to her guests. "They'll go away."

"Gypsies," the Professor of Sauces said. "They are everywhere."

Elza motioned to the waitstaff, and the head waiter left the restaurant to try and chase the children away. The children made faces at him when he approached them and began running in circles around him. They turned it into a game. They tapped against the glass when they got behind him. They laughed and stuck their tongues out at Elza and her guests.

"Why are you behaving so badly today?" Elza spoke sternly, but she also smiled at them and wagged her finger. "Leave now, or I'll chase you with my broom and then you'll be sorry!"

The children, the same three boys she had seen at the flower girl's home, pointed at her and made faces. They stopped running in circles and put their faces close to the window.

"Hello, restaurant lady," the littlest of them called out. "Can you give us money today? Give us something to eat!"

"Come back later," she said. "Not right now."

The Headwaiter started to push them roughly. Elza tapped the glass to catch his attention and shook her head at him. The boys stepped away from the window and began cursing at him. Elza tapped the glass again, and they began cursing at her as well. Then they suddenly stopped and turned around. They walked away in deep conversation, as though nothing had happened. The head waiter looked through the window and shrugged. Elza and her guests watched as one of the children picked up a cigarette butt and lit it with a wooden match he produced from the pocket of his shabby shorts. The boys took turns smoking it as they headed toward the Centrum.

Elza turned to her instructors and apologized again. She pointed at the magazine.

"I want to bring this man here to review Tulip," she said. "Will you help me do that?"

The two instructors looked at one another and hesitated.

"My dear," said the Professor of Sauces, "don't you want to think about that a little? To invite this man here might not be in your best interests."

"Yes," said the Professor of Meats. "I agree. It seems like a hasty decision. He's not the sort of man you should trifle with."

Elza shook her head and waved a hand.

"I am not afraid," she said. She motioned to a few framed articles on her walls. "We've been reviewed in magazines before."

"My dear," said the Professor of Sauces as he looked at the articles around them. Not wanting to offend, he thought for a moment before continuing. "Yes, you have been reviewed, but this isn't a local paper, or even a national magazine. You are talking about a good review *and* winning the Silver Ladle. But, my dear, I must speak plainly. These are the French. This is *Le Gourmand* we're talking about! They are *the* last word on haute cuisine. I don't want to say that you are delusional, but perhaps you might temper your enthusiasm? If only a little? Lovely as your restaurant is, tasty as the food is, you might really embarrass yourself."

The Professor of Meats nodded gravely and wiped his mouth with his napkin. He twisted it before absentmindedly dropping it on the floor instead of back on his lap. Elza watched him. She noticed three stains on the cloth arranged in the pattern of a clover. She remembered the look on their plates. The food had been polished off of them. This is it, she decided. This is the challenge she was looking for. This is the challenge that would help her out of her apathy. This would help her escape from being second-rate.

"Gentlemen," she said, "I've never been afraid to stick my neck out. I'm certain I can win this man's belly over. All I'm asking is if you will help me bring him here."

The Professor of Sauces shook his head, but the Professor of Meats, perhaps because he was a professor of meats, because he handled cleavers and skewers, because he cooked over open pits and open flames, because he, too, liked getting his way—the Professor of Meats smacked his hand on the table as if it were the rump end of a butchered calf.

"I will help you," he said. "We will both see what we can do to get in touch with him."

The Professor of Sauces rolled his eyes.

Four

Several weeks had passed since the instructors' visit to Tulip, and Elza's argument with her sous-chef over brined pork and marriage proposals had evolved into something entirely different. It was clear to both of them that they had reached the end of their romantic involvement. Elza placed the remainder of his belongings in a pile in her front room; but as he had stopped visiting, he never came to collect them, and they sat there. They never spoke again about their quarrels. In fact, they stopped speaking at all except when absolutely necessary. Still, in the very beginning of their separation, at night, when her dreams of escaping awoke her, Elza reached over to the empty side of her bed and could not help feeling alone. She thought about calling him, but something inside her would not allow her to do it. She convinced herself it was not a real relationship she had shared with the Sous-Chef. She had known all along she did not want to marry him. It might have been cruel, but she admitted to herself that he had only been a distraction, a bad habit, and Elza decided that she needed to wean herself from thinking about him. She should behave as a smoker might with a pack of cigarettes.

So, remembering the fortitude it took to quit smoking, Elza steeled herself to her walks and to the idea of only seeing the Sous-Chef at the restaurant, and it turned out that eventually she did not miss him at all. How odd, she thought to herself. How odd that they had spent nearly three years together and she had never felt sentimental about him, wondered about him, nor had she felt herself changed in any way.

Elza was fine with the new arrangement. She enjoyed her freedom. She was glad the Sous-Chef remained at the restaurant and continued to work. It all would have worked out with Elza perfectly, except that for his part, the Sous-Chef was miserable. He was becoming surlier and surlier as the days passed. He grew pouty. At work in the kitchen, he openly sneered at her. He looked up at the ceiling when she spoke to him. He turned his back on her before she finished sentences. He still managed the daily operations of the kitchen, still handled the day-to-day cooking, but it was all handled coolly. Elza could not help but be affected by this new behavior. She was honestly flummoxed by it. In spite of the marriage proposals, she had always figured he must have felt the same about her as she did about him. She never considered that he was genuinely hurt. Confused by him, unsure of how to proceed, instead of confronting him, she found herself snapping instead at the new pastry chef, Dora, a lean young woman with dramatic eye shadow and bouncing yellow locks. Elza had noticed that Dora had recently begun smiling a little too easily at the Sous-Chef, and she did not like it.

"I can't tell if I'm jealous or just territorial," she confided to her friend, the widow Eva, who visited one day for lunch.

The older woman was licking a dessert spoon. She looked up at Elza.

"Darling, you'll just have to get rid of her," she said.

"I can't!" Elza said and pointed at Eva's dish. "The dessert business has picked up since she got here. She makes the pies and the torte. She's infusing her crusts with plum brandy. The customers love them. And her crepes are simply excellent. They're so light. She uses club soda in the batter. You should see her in the kitchen, whisking away like a machine. She does it all by hand! No, I can't fire her. She's an excellent pastry chef."

Eva dipped her spoon in hand-whipped cream and licked it again. "It is very good cake," she agreed. "She makes this, you say?"

Elza looked at the empty dish and nodded.

"It's my second helping," Eva said. "I've been ordering them and taking them with me the last few weeks. My dresses are tightening around my hips. You know how long it takes me to stuff myself into my clothing in the morning? I'm like a sausage these days. I take it back. You can't fire her. Eating her desserts is the most fun my old mouth has had this year."

Elza shrugged and ate from her own dish. *It is good. Maybe a touch sweet.*

The women reflected quietly a moment. Suddenly, Eva smiled. She was remembering an incident from her youth involving an itinerant worker that her father had had to deal with when he discovered that his daughter's much younger mouth had been having inappropriate fun behind a tool shed. That was the summer when they had rebuilt the fence. Her father had discovered the affair but instead of blowing his top and losing his daughter, he had made sure the worker worked. A shovel, an obstinate mule, a stack of posts, and two kilometers were all he had needed. The younger Eva had waited for hours at their predetermined spot only to find that when her worker met her—three hours later than he had promised—he was filthy and tired and not in the mood to fondle the boss's daughter.

She had smacked him for making a fool of her and that had been enough to chase him off, to make him leave that very night.

Perhaps the same thing might help Elza with her situation, she thought. So, Eva smiled and announced what she had been thinking.

"You should double the number of cakes she makes every day! Double the number of crepes, while you're at it. Expand! Open a pastry shop. Double everything! They're young, darling. If you really want to keep her away from him, then you would do best to keep her up to her elbows in cream and lady fingers. Keep her up to her knees in batter. Make her as sweaty as possible. No time for eye shadow when there's work to be done."

Elza laughed at the thought of Dora's eye shadow being ruined. She liked the idea. She also understood the logic to it, and so within a few days boxed crepes and cakes were added to the menu. Customers loved the new additions and orders took off. In fact, people were now visiting the restaurant just to carry pastries out. Elza had to add a second phone line for customers to place orders. Dora was loaded down with work. When she complained that she needed help, Elza offered her the choice of an assistant or a substantial raise. The young woman considered it for a moment and chose the raise.

Under the pretext of streamlining her production, Elza also moved the pastry station to the other end of the kitchen, as far away from the Sous-Chef as was possible. *This should take care of things*, Elza thought.

In regard to the restaurant's operations, the new dessert business was such a success that Elza saw her profits increase fifteen percent that month, even factoring in Dora's raise. To celebrate, Elza closed the restaurant early one evening and she and her employees had a party. All of them, that is, except the Sous-Chef, who insisted he had to go home to his mother, and Dora, who stayed only an hour before slipping out.

In regard to keeping Dora occupied and away from the Sous-Chef, however, the plan was an utter failure. A disaster, really. It only emboldened the two of them. The young woman had nerve. Her eye shadow remained perfect—if one could call bruised-looking perfect. And perspiration had not done anything to slow her down. It only made her appear dewy and seemed to make her ever more slippery. Elza kept an eye open from her office because the girl used any excuse to slide across the kitchen to the Sous-Chef's station like some kind of ardent grass snake hunting for breakfast.

"Has anyone seen my whisk?" she would hear Dora calling out before spying her slipping over to the Sous-Chef and looking for the damned thing behind pans and pots of boiling water. Elza noticed that her hands caressed the Sous-Chef's back as she walked past him.

And the Sous-Chef encouraged the young woman! He would stop whatever he was doing and make a big show of helping her look. All the line cooks would stop what they were doing and help look also. This detestable young woman had caused three grown men to hop around the kitchen like crickets, all looking for her whisk, giggling like children because she was young and pretty and dewy and bruised-looking and was paying attention to them. All the while Elza knew that Dora probably had the damned thing in her front pocket, and of course she was correct in thinking this. Inevitably, she would spot the Sous-Chef with his hands down Dora's apron front—playfully, of course. Oh-so-innocently—fondling her in front of a cooking stew—looking for her whisk. Dora would look up at him with her speckled eyes—eyes with no color, eyes with every color—and she would shake her head.

"It's not there, silly," she'd whisper in a breathy voice. "How would it ever fit?"

And being a man, this nitwitted game and that nitwitted little-girl voice of hers seemed enough to send him into a single-minded trance. The Sous-Chef would peek over his shoulder to check if Elza was watching. *Damn right I'm watching*, Elza thought. Then he would act as if he hadn't seen her glaring at them, and he would take another step toward Dora—though he was practically pressed against her already—and the young woman, who was quite good at playing her part, Elza noted, would take the smallest step back and brush against the warm stove. She'd jump with a start and launch herself, innocently, into his arms.

"Oh! It's hot!"

The Sous-Chef feigned concern and spun her around to examine her bottom for burns.

"Don't hurt yourself," he said.

Meanwhile, the line cooks watched and surreptitiously licked their lips. They cursed the Sous-Chef's skill with women, stirred their pots, glanced at one another, and then looked sideways toward Elza's office.

And to top it off, the Sous-Chef always did find the whisk hidden in some ridiculous spot under her apron. He would reach *under* her clothing and pull it from wherever Dora had hidden it.

"I guess it fits after all," he would chide and smile with those perfect straight teeth.

"Now how did that get there?" Dora would nearly scream and grab the whisk from him and brandish it like a sword. She'd begin poking him playfully with it, over and over, telling him in a singsong voice, like a fey lion tamer, to back off. Telling him *he* should be whipped . . . but good.

Elza had reached her wit's end.

"Tomorrow I'll buy you seventeen whisks," she shouted. "Right now we need more crepes!" A hush fell over the kitchen. Dora returned to her station.

Elza tried to feel otherwise, but she felt betrayed by the young man's interest. She could not help but grimace at the way he watched Dora cross the kitchen toward him. She could not help but grimace at the way *he* crossed the kitchen and offered to help Dora with her prep work, to help her whip cream, or to help her wipe batter off her dainty nose. Elza found herself grimacing a lot and not doing much else, but she kept her mouth shut lest she show the Sous-Chef any kind of jealousy. She remained in her office, but she stuck her head out her door as often as she could to bark orders and dampen any burgeoning affection—never mind how exhausting it was keeping the two separated, never mind that their nether regions were seemingly magnetized.

And of course, none of this was helping Elza reach her own goals. She could not follow up on calls like she wanted to because she was always watching out for the young chefs in heat in her kitchen. Her ennui, silenced when her new project began, had bloomed again. She had fallen off task, and it seemed the less she worked now on finding the Critic, and the more she worked on keeping the younger people apart, the more depressed she became. She stopped caring. She stopped putting on makeup. Eventually, she even stopped showering.

After a second month slipped away, two months after she thought she had started on her new path, in order to win herself peace of mind, she invited the Sous-Chef back to her flat for drinks one evening after they had closed up. She made the invitation in front of everyone, in front of the line cooks, in front of the Dishwasher, and in front of Dora.

"We need to talk about the state of the kitchen," she said cryptically.

The line cooks shifted. The Sous-Chef looked at Elza and when he thought she was distracted, he looked at Dora and shrugged. The young woman scowled at him and turned away.

Elza was pleased with herself, pleased with the effect. She did not want him back, but she wanted to make peace with him. If she could get him up to her flat, get a drink or two into him, talk a little, he might loosen up. They had not had a conversation in over a month. He agreed to follow her, and after they closed the restaurant and sent everyone home, they walked awkwardly alongside each other until they reached her building. The Sous-Chef followed her inside her foyer as he had many times before, and Elza even considered that the evening might lead to something affectionate, something that might bridge the growing rift between them. However, whereas previously he might have caressed the small of her back or touched her shoulder, his arms were close to his sides and he looked around the foyer with disgust.

"I never noticed how old and dingy this place was," he said. "Why do they only fix the facades?"

Elza looked around, genuinely surprised by this remark. "Is it?"

"Can't you see that?" He pointed at a corner. It was black with years of accumulated dirt and soot. "Depressing. I'm looking at one of those new flats being built near the shopping mall. They're going to be very modern. American-style kitchens and radiant floors."

"You're going to buy a flat?" Elza asked. She was surprised to hear this. It was a dream of his that she'd heard him speak of often.

"I have finally talked my mother into giving me the weekend garden to sell. She's too old to enjoy it. My sister and I don't use it. We'll split the money. There's also the money my father left behind. If I sell my old car and take a loan, I'll have enough . . . for that and other things."

"That's nice," Elza said and could not understand why she felt uneasy. Perhaps it had something to do with the confidence with which he had just announced his plans. It sounded as though he was making things happen. Elza wondered if he could have grown so quickly in the past month. She wondered if she had been smothering him. Her stomach stirred. She grabbed his hand and pulled him to the lift. It had been replaced since he had last visited.

"Let me show you something modern," she said. "You'll love it."

The elevator door opened. The Sous-Chef laughed.

"That's silly," he said. "They leave the dirt and old tiles, but they upgrade the elevators to look like spaceships? This is exactly why I'm buying a flat in a new building. These old ones are too much trouble. They should tear them all down."

Elza ignored the comment and stepped into the elevator. It did look like a spaceship, she thought. She pushed her floor number and they went up in silence. He followed her to her door, and once inside her flat, the Sous-Chef would not take off his shoes or jacket. He sat at her kitchen table and pulled a pack of cigarettes from his shirt pocket. He lit one and smoked. He did not offer one to her. She brought his bag of things out and poured them both drinks. They were quiet, both of them behaving as though he were a guest, a stranger.

"Are you sleeping with Dora?" she asked suddenly, when it was clear he would not speak and she had grown tired of watching him exhale blue smoke into her kitchen.

She wanted to kick herself for coming out with it so quickly, but she wanted to know. The Sous-Chef did not answer right away. He smirked and blew a cloud of smoke and then drank from his tumbler. He looked at her. "So that's what this is about!" He laughed. Elza noted that he did not answer her question.

"I want you to stop torturing me," Elza said. "I haven't done anything to deserve this sort of behavior from you."

The Sous-Chef scoffed. He was wide-eyed. "Are you serious?"

"What have I done?" Elza asked. "I've been kind and honest with you."

"Will you marry me?" the Sous-Chef asked.

"No," she said. "Is that what all this is about? How many times do you need to hear it? Don't be silly. I do not want to marry you. And I want you to stop whatever you're doing or planning to do with my pastry chef."

The Sous-Chef took another drag from his cigarette and exhaled all the smoke he could into her kitchen. He finished his drink and rose from his seat simultaneously. He shook his head.

"You're a real piece of work," he said. "A crazy piece of work."

"Keep her on her side of the kitchen," Elza warned him. Her voice cracked a little.

"That's ridiculous!" he shouted. "It's not a big enough kitchen. And how do you expect *your* sous-chef to ignore *your* pastry chef?"

"You're playing with your jobs," she threatened.

He snorted. She had hoped the threat would scare him, but he did not look afraid.

"You can't fire us," he said. "You need us. You would break the kitchen if you fired either of us. It'd take too long to find decent replacements in this town. And you're too good to cook in the kitchen yourself any more. You won't fire us."

"You want to try it and see?" Elza was out of her seat and at him like a terrier. He took a step back. She stared at him until he averted his eyes. "I have more burns on my hands than you'll ever know. I've cut every finger I have more than a dozen times. You stupid little shit. I invented and cooked every meal on that menu. I taught you everything! Just keep her on her side of the kitchen. I have enough on my mind without having to worry about you going and getting her pregnant. Her pastries are flying out the door and our profits are up, and that's what I'm most interested in. I have loans to pay back and responsibilities that you just don't understand."

The Sous-Chef's mouth fell open. Elza shook her head.

"I mean, I don't want you—"

He cursed and turned. He flicked the cigarette out of the kitchen window. Elza tried to grab his hand but he pulled it away.

"Just stay away from her," she said weakly. "This is still my restaurant!"

He laughed at that and left. "It might be your restaurant," he said as he walked out, "but it's *our* kitchen."

And from that moment, the air at the restaurant between Elza and the Sous-Chef grew from uncomfortably tense to ill-willed and finally to intolerable. The animosity between them made its way around the kitchen, and soon enough, everyone was seething. The kitchen, it seemed, was broken anyway. The line cooks were tense. The Dishwasher was tense. The waiters were tense. The flower girl noticed it first when a waiter barked at her for getting in the way. The children noticed it next when Elza herself scolded them harshly and told them to leave the front of her restaurant and never come back. The boys cursed at her, which led Elza to actually chase them a bit. Finally, customers also began to notice the frustration during their visits. Maybe it was the snappy waiter, or maybe it was something unsettling in the food itself—an angry hand unable to control how much pepper fell into a soup or how much salt was rubbed into a chicken. Whatever it was, something was causing the customers to look over their shoulders apprehensively while they ate and then to leave quickly.

"Indigestion is unforgivable, what?" her customers told each other.

Even their beloved Elza seemed different. She could no longer hide her unhappiness. She did not smile so readily at her visitors. Her hands did not flutter. She still tried occasionally. She pulled a greasy strand of hair behind her ear and stretched her lips, but there was a false start to it. The customers looked around the dining room and saw that the mirrors hadn't been polished and they whispered to themselves.

"Maybe she's overworked."

"I think she's just getting old. Have you taken a good look at her recently? Let's eat someplace else next time. I can get Chicken Paprika at home."

And they did. That easily. It was only a restaurant, after all. And Elza's numbers plateaued after a twenty-three-percent rise and then dipped. Her gentlemen stopped calling as often. After a waiter insisted he take off his helmet and holster his weapon, the Motorcycle Officer stopped coming in entirely. He was the one who had come in every day for four years for lunch! The Professor of Humanities was next. He finally had enough when instead of Hollandaithe thauthe a waiter presented him with a bowl of thour cream, would not take it back, and even made fun of his lisp. The waiter told him he would pour the thour cream on his head before he'd serve him Hollandaithe thauthe again.

Elza still thought about the Critic. She carried the tattered magazine with her everywhere she went. Her former instructors had proven to be useful and when she contacted them they said they were getting close to tracking him down and that it would only be a matter of time.

"A few weeks, perhaps," the Professor of Meats said. "We're waiting for him to call back. You're actually in luck because the magazine is interested in expanding readership eastward. They're looking to cover restaurants in new Europe."

Elza was sitting in her office. She nodded and peeked into the kitchen.

"Wonderful," she said. "Just wonderful."

"This is a great opportunity. Just keep everything the way you have it, and everything should be fine," the Professor of Meats continued. "The pork loin is a guaranteed winner. The desserts are fabulous."

Elza laughed loudly. She tried to make it sound like a happy laugh. She made it even louder. She wanted her employees to hear she was feeling just fine.

"We're in tip-top shape," she shouted into the phone. "No problems here. He'll have the meal of his life."

Dora was openly canoodling with the Sous-Chef now. Elza really would have fired both of them—she wanted to—but she felt if she was indeed close to the Critic visiting, if the instructors' leads were as good as they sounded, she really could not afford to lose them just yet. They were at a critical moment. Maybe after the Critic had visited. She hated to admit it to herself, but the Sous-Chef was correct, it would take too long to break in two new chefs. It would take too long for new chefs to learn the recipes. She cursed herself for having given up the day-to-day cooking. She lamented ever having handed so many of the operations to the Sous-Chef. She could always help out in the kitchen, but she knew that they had grown into a unit without her, and she would just disturb whatever dynamic had grown among them.

Elza left her office and walked to Dora's station to examine a stack of crepes warming over a pot of steam. Dora was powdering a sheet of rolled crepes with confectionary sugar. The sweet smell lingered around the station. The two women smiled at one another, but they could just as easily have scratched each other's eyes out.

Elza could not understand it. When she hired Dora, she envisioned them becoming like sisters. She wanted to be a mentor to the younger woman. She should never have allowed it to begin. She should have punished Dora's behavior from the start.

And there were plenty of other men at the restaurant to make eyes at. Why not flirt with one of them? In fact, the Dishwasher was available. Elza looked at the man. He was short and unkempt. He was stout. He was a hard worker, though. He worked like a machine, endless cycles of washing and drying. Hot water blasted from his hose's nozzle. Going back to his station was like walking into a sauna, but he handled it like a science. Every plate was organized and sterile. Elza had even allowed him to take care of the linens for extra money. He was worth his weight in gold, Elza thought. Even the widow, Eva, had seen him once and remarked on him to Elza.

"Who's that funny-looking little man?"

"What? Him?" Elza asked her and thought she recognized a lascivious grin on the older woman's face. "Control yourself. That's the Dishwasher."

The widow Eva's face did not change. She clucked her tongue and sucked on a crepe.

"Oh, is it now," she'd said. "Is he married?"

Dora did not seem to see him that way, though. She always crinkled her nose at him when he smiled at her or told her she looked pretty.

"Ah . . . it stinks back here!" Dora would say as she dropped off a baking pan or a dish of butter. She whipped her curls around and hurried away, leaving only a trace of shampoo in her wake.

The Dishwasher laughed good-naturedly at her, and when he did he shook like a sea monster or some lost bastard of Poseidon's. When he shook, he sent droplets of water through the air. The droplets were warm and salty. They came from his own mess of hair—loose black tendrils that fell over his eyebrows.

"Ah, little Dora," he would say, "that's the smell of a real man!"

Why not carry on with him? Elza thought. There'd be no trouble there.

The line cooks were laughing. Elza walked around their stations and they grew quiet. She stopped beside the Sous-Chef and glared at him, but he ignored her. She stood for a few moments and willed him to look at her, but he would not. In fact, he walked away. While she watched, he crossed the kitchen and stood beside Dora. He put his hand on the small of her back. She responded by putting her head against his chest. Elza felt sick. The pair talked in low voices and began laughing. He helped her stir a fresh batch of batter. That is, he held his hand over hers and they stirred the same wooden spoon . . . together. Elza returned to her office quickly before the line cooks could notice her face flushing. *Why not flirt with one of the waiters?* she thought as she picked up the phone. All of them were single. Why wouldn't Dora flirt with one of them?

The cause of all this tension in the kitchen was certainly not lost on the other employees. Despite their years of careful coordination of their affair, every employee at Tulip knew of Elza and the Sous-Chef's relationship. It did not take a genius to realize that Elza's increasingly stern demeanor correlated to the Sous-Chef's and Dora's increasing physical attraction. What surprised everyone else in the kitchen was how long Elza had allowed it. What surprised everyone was that Elza had rewarded the girl by giving her so much more responsibility and pay. Instead of tossing her out on her ear, she had Dora filling colorful to-go boxes with crepes and tortes. In trying to smother Dora's passion, Elza had lost face. So now, when they weren't arguing or fuming at the stress in the kitchen, her employees were tittering openly and beginning to shirk their duties.

"Anything goes with this lady," the first line cook—the Saucier—said to the second. "Screw it."

The Sous-Chef knew that the others knew, but he said nothing. As far as he was concerned, he was moving on to greater opportunities, waiting for the moment when he could escape from Elza and her restaurant entirely.

"I wasted three years on her," he complained to his mother and sister when Elza had refused his last proposal. "Three years because I thought she loved me and would come around."

His mother and sister nodded.

"These things are never a waste," his mother said and patted his hand. "You learned a lot. She gave you a lot. It's a journey."

"Bah," he said. "I'm done with journeys. First I'll see how things go with Dora, then I'll buy my flat and open my own restaurant," he said. "I'll take the Dishwasher with me."

"That sounds good, dearie," his mother said. "You can do it. You can do anything."

"I'm thirty," he said. "I've got to get my life started."

So, the Sous-Chef accepted the line cooks' ribbing when Elza was out of earshot with a grimace of controlled anger. The way he saw it, he was already gone.

However, the two lesser cooks were small-minded and relentless in their attacks.

"You stopped kneading the missus's backside then?" the Saucier asked.

The Sous-Chef didn't answer.

"You stuffing the little one now?"

The men were laughing. The Sous-Chef looked up at them threateningly. They were coarse—not trained chefs, only lost peasants who had stumbled onto a city job. However, their faces wore the expressions of conquering marauders. They behaved as if they had outwitted all of society by holding onto petty little kitchen jobs.

"He asked if you was stuffing the little one." The second line cook asked the question again and looked over at Dora's backside. "She's a right piece of work, yeah? I like those black eyes she's always got. I've never known a woman to do that. It'd look like a mess on my old lady, but on her it looks real good."

The Sous-Chef slammed a cleaver down onto a cutting board. He eyeballed the line cook.

"Keep your dirty little mouth shut," he threatened. "Shut it or you'll be out of a job."

This particular line cook was a lowlife Elza had hired over his protests. The Sous-Chef had taken an immediate dislike to the man. Besides being coarse he was just trouble. He seemed too at ease, too much like a criminal. But Elza had shrugged it off the way she always shrugged him off. She liked the fact that the man came from the country and knew how to butcher meat perfectly. He could slice away fat as though he had been a surgeon. He could cut through fascia gingerly and leave nothing behind but a lean piece of meat. He could even gut a rabbit if he needed to.

"Fire me!" the line cook smirked. "That's rich. I don't believe your dear mommy would let you."

The two men glared at each other. The Sous-Chef knew it was true. He felt the cleaver in his hand and raised it threateningly.

"Keep it down," he warned. "If she hears you, we're both done for."

The line cook smirked. "You're a cunt. I've always thought so, and I don't see any reason not to say so now. A gigolo cunt. You'll be out of here before I am. I can promise you that. You and your pet raccoon."

The Dishwasher and the Saucier stopped what they were doing and watched the interaction. They shook their heads. They might all have had years of experience together. They might have understood the menu. They might all have been shown by Elza how to prepare each item from scratch, have established a routine, but it had all been for naught. The men in Elza's kitchen began threatening to castrate one another nightly—the Sous-Chef and his line cook, the Saucier and the Dishwasher—everywhere these angry men turned, an angrier man was standing next to him and brandishing cutlery at his bits. And all of them knew that mentioning the Sous-Chef's affair with Elza or Dora was the easiest way to stir up trouble.

Five

He's arriving next week. We did it!"

The words coming through Elza's phone carried the weight of an unexpected thunderclap behind them and caused her to sit upright and grip her armrest. She simultaneously caught a glimpse of herself in a mirror and saw the wide-eyed shock on her face. She also noticed how much she had stopped caring about her appearance. Her hair was greasy looking. She could have stood a facial. She wondered how long the stress had been festering on her face. While there weren't quite half-moons underneath her eyes, she noticed a shadow she had never seen before. The thunderclap of a message jarred her. She would fix all of the things around her that needed fixing as soon as she got off the phone. Finally, she was getting somewhere. Finally, she might be able to open the throttle on her engines. Finally. She looked up at her office ceiling and mouthed a thank-you.

The Professor of Meats was still talking to her. She turned her attention back to listening. She was flabbergasted, still bowled over; her breath was taken away from her. He was relaying in full now the story of how they had hunted the Critic down—how, working in shifts on the project, the pair of them, together, had stalked and flushed him out into the open.

"The man doesn't rest," the Professor of Meats said. "We missed him by a day in Gothenburg. He had just left for Brussels. When we called the restaurant he was supposed to be visiting, they told us he had changed his mind—some kind of emergency, they said—and gone back instead to Paris. They were very angry. They had made a black truffle soufflé that had taken them weeks to perfect. They spent a lot of time and money on it, so I guess it's understandable they were upset. Very inconsiderate of him. Anyway, we tried the magazine again, but they wouldn't give us his number right away, and when they finally did a few days later, after I literally begged them, he had left town to visit his mother. So, we tried him in Italy, and then we lost track of him for a few days. We think he was on to the Netherlands next, or London, but then he was back in Paris, or maybe it was the other way around. Quite a busy fellow! Finally, we decided upon calling him at his home every evening until we reached him, and we caught him late one night, a little before midnight. He was put out by that considerably. He actually shouted at me. I must say, Elza, I'm not used to being shouted at, but I stood it for your sake. What choice did I have? His editor told me that this is a special issue they're working on, after all—their first thorough look at restaurants in the former *Eastern Bloc*. He said it just like that, *Eastern Bloc*, as if it were Fiji or Kathmandu. I didn't realize people still used the term.

"Anyway, when I finally got through to him, after he stopped yelling at me, he asked me to stop harassing him, and hung up. But when I called him early the next morning—early, dear, before I'd even breakfasted—well, he was in no better spirits, I can tell you that, but at least he heard me out. He said he'd spoken to his editor, and he agreed to visit if we agreed to stop calling. I agreed and gave him our details. The editor called back a day later with an itinerary in place. He agreed that an article covering traditional Hungarian kitchens would be interesting to their readers. He also liked the fact that your restaurant serves traditional cuisine in a fine-dining atmosphere. We assured him that you were an artist! That Tulip was not fusion, but something authentic and inward-looking. We also told him you were haute-cuisine and should be given consideration for the Silver Ladle. I must be honest with you here, my dear, but the editor scoffed at that. I ignored it. He'll see! So, anyway, the Critic will arrive at the school next week, and after a tour we'll bring him directly to you. He'll be our summer guest at Lake Balaton afterward and we've arranged plenty of time for him to visit the thermals. You should think about joining us for a weekend or so as well. What do you say to that?"

Elza had stood up and pushed her chair away from her. She was pacing around her office. She was speechless. She looked at the Critic's picture in the latest issue of *Le Gourmand* and then looked at herself in a mirror again. She straightened her hair and pressed her lips together. The only thing she could think to do was practice her smile. She tilted her head and retracted her lips. She did not think of the broken kitchen or the fact that the Sliver Ladle was as far out of reach as a Michelin star. All she could think to do at that moment was offer her hand to the imaginary man in front of her.

What is the matter with me? she thought. There was hardly any time left to plan. She was at the threshold of accomplishing something monumental in her medium-size city—something that might establish her reputation internationally. In an instant everything in her world came into sharp focus. She had a purpose as clear and sharp as a glass shard. Like the new capitalists around her, the rest of the burgeoning middle class, like the merchants in their boutiques, the managers in their telecom firms, the young bankers sprouting in the new banks, Elza knew she had an audit to contend with. She thought about the resources she needed to see this project to completion. She was able, in that moment of pacing, with a deadline hanging over her head, and only a moment after smiling and offering her hand to nobody, she was able to determine what her next course of action should be, exactly what needed to happen. *Why can't it just always be like this?* she thought. Why, so often, did it seem that she had to muddle from cause to effect, from half-baked decision to tentative action, with no recipe or anything else to guide her? Just muddling. Throwing things into a pot and hoping they'll get along. But then there was suddenly this! Why, this was practically heroic, she thought. Here she was, suddenly alive and steering her life in the direction it needed to go.

"Elza? Are you there?" the Professor of Meats asked at the other end of the line.

"Yes. Yes! This is wonderful—absolutely wonderful! Thank you so much. The kitchen is ready. We're all waiting for him."

"Good, good. You should have nothing to worry about. We are both so happy for you, my dear. It will be a fine distinction for you and for the old school. You certainly have worked hard all these years and deserve your success. You deserve to have people know it. No reason we can't show the West a thing or two—show them what a Magyar kitchen can produce. Let them have a taste of *Eastern Bloc* cuisine."

"Yes, indeed!" Elza said good-bye and hung up. She peeked out at the kitchen with fresh, purposeful eyes. Everything would be fixed—even this chaotic kitchen.

But what chaos! Dirty pots and pans were strewn over countertops. Too many abandoned dish towels were tossed carelessly on top of oven ranges. A trash bin was overflowing. There was a puddle of congealed fat on the floor. The door to the alley was open and the line cooks were standing outside smoking. The Sous-Chef should really have been keeping them in line. But where was the Sous-Chef? He was helping Dora prepare a batch of sour cherries for pies instead.

He stirred the cherries while Dora poured the sugar in, and something in the way they interacted struck Elza and rendered her light-headed with anger. She marched into the kitchen and moved a dishrag from a range. She watched them speaking softly to each other, speaking gently to each other. Ten years of hard work had brought her this? Ten years of scraping pots and gutting chickens and getting burned by pans that spit hot oil at her, of giving up a normal life, had led her to this: no family, no love, no respect, a filthy kitchen, and an ex-lover stirring a pot of cherries with an attractive younger woman? Elza did not think of herself as an envious woman, but right then she wanted to break a few dishes. But she also realized that she had gotten herself in to this mess. *Life requires constant effort*, she realized, *constant vigilance. I have not been vigilant. I let everything burn while playing make-believe*. She knew that to proceed, she would have to control her anger, she would have to choose wisely . . . and she almost did! She felt herself calming down enough to project a level-headed authority. She was on the brink of reaching a level of detached intelligence, akin to a mindful monk, but as she was about to open her mouth and speak to her employees in a mindful, purposeful way, she took a step and skidded on the puddle of congealed fat. Her right leg slipped out and took off on an unaccustomed trajectory from under her while her left one buckled. Then she landed on her backside with her hand in the thick mess. *Her* thick mess. All of it, hers. She pulled her hand away from the fat and stared at it. Her hand glistened and smelled rancid. Chicken fat—days old—from a pan that had been carelessly carried, that had tipped slightly on the way to the dish station. This was the worst part: nobody had seen or heard her fall. She was invisible in her own kitchen. The line chefs were still chatting and smoking in the back. The Sous-Chef was still talking softly with Dora over the cherries, and the Dishwasher had his back turned while he folded napkins.

Sitting there on the messy floor of her kitchen, in her restaurant, at the age of forty-eight, without a person in the world, not even her immediate world, who cared about whether she stood or fell, succeeded or failed, lived or died, had money in the bank or not, Elza succumbed to a fiery rage. *If I have to set all of their asses on fire, this is my restaurant, and I'll make it ready.*

It was at this moment that the hair on the back of Dora's neck began to stand. Dora shivered now while she and the Sous-Chef rendered the steaming pot of cherries and sugar. She turned to see Elza standing in the middle of the kitchen with a contorted mouth, a perplexed brow, and her hand raised up like a statue. Her face had gone bright red. Really, the only thing missing was smoke billowing out of her ears. Elza looked like a stovetop coffee pot about to explode. Precisely like that.

The poor girl, as good a pastry chef as she was, was no match for the brewing storm. She might as well have been a cream puff lost at stormy sea or a deviled egg tossed in front of an approaching steamroller.

"Get out of my sight!" Elza shouted at her and pointed to the exit. "Get out! Get out! Get out!"

Dora tried to make herself disappear behind the Sous-Chef. She managed enough so that only her nose and smoky eyes peeked out behind him, and indeed at that moment she looked very much like an apprehensive raccoon.

The line cooks heard Elza and peeked inside. They spotted the fat stain on her uniform, surmised the situation, and quickly put out their cigarettes and came back indoors. They shut the alley door behind them. The Dishwasher dropped a napkin when he heard the shout and instinctively reached for a knife. He spun on his heels and crouched down, ready for action, ready to take apart the intruder he thought had broken in.

Outside, in the dining room, the Headwaiter heard the shout, but tried to ignore it. He smiled at the customers and the other waiters and offered a glass of wine. The customers heard the shout also. Many of them were in the middle of chewing or swallowing or bringing their forks to their mouths. They stopped what they were doing. The Postal Inspector raised an eyebrow and stood up. He tried to look through the doors to see what was happening in the kitchen. He looked over at the Motorcycle Officer, who had resumed eating at Tulip—sans helmet, and pistol holstered—when he realized lunch really wasn't the same anywhere else. The pair of them, being the only uniformed officials in the restaurant and therefore representing the state's authority, stood up and made their way to the kitchen doors.

The Headwaiter ran in front of them. He knew what a mess the kitchen had become and did not want anyone to find out.

"All is well," he said. "All is just fine. They're only having a little spat. A little chef's spat. Culinary differences, you know. Artistes!"

"That was Elza shouting," the Postal Inspector said. "I recognized the voice."

"I did too," said the Motorcycle Officer and he nodded at the other customers. "I recognized it as well. I also heard it first."

The Headwaiter shook his head. "Gentlemen, everything is all right. Please return to your meals. They'll get cold."

It took a bit of cajoling and promises of free desserts, but eventually the men sat down. They introduced themselves and moved their dishes over to a larger table where they finished their meal together.

And back in the kitchen, with all eyes on her and her kitchen brigade wondering what she would do, Elza remembered the big picture. The Critic was coming. *Le Gourmand* would review her Tulip.

"I've reached a decision and I'm going to give you a choice," she announced in a lower register of voice.

The Sous-Chef turned fully around to face her and puffed out his chest. The line cooks jabbed each other with their elbows and sniggered at him. The Dishwasher came out from his station still holding the knife out in front of him.

"What kind of choice?" the Sous-Chef asked.

"This isn't working," Elza said and looked at all of them. "None of this is working. I've spent the last ten years building this restaurant from nothing, and I've received word that *Le Gourmand* will be here next week." She looked at Dora and the Sous-Chef. "Now, I'm going to give you both the choice of staying on in your jobs for another week and helping me serve him a meal he'll never forget, or leaving my restaurant today. Right now. If you stay and do a good job, do everything I ask, I'll give you each severance pay. If you choose to leave right now, you'll get nothing. You're both fired, but I'd be lying if I said I couldn't use you a little longer."

"Why would I stay?" Dora blurted out without hesitation. She stuck her head out further from behind the Sous-Chef. Now *her* face was puffy and red. Her eyes had welled up with tears that made her mascara and eye shadow blotchy. The smell of her sugared cherries still hung in the air, but now they were beginning to burn, and the hint of burnt sugar was just starting to manifest itself.

The line cooks laughed at the image of her small yellow head and black eyes sticking out, but Dora paid them no mind. She was indignant at having been yelled at, and had reached the conclusion herself that she'd had enough. The truth of the matter was that she had been ready to leave after her first month on the job. In fact, she had been urging the Sous-Chef to join her for weeks now. She had her own plans and money already—from industrious parents who wanted her to get a little training before opening her own concern. The only reason she had stayed was because the Sous-Chef was helping her get over her fears of being young and inexperienced. Now, she was ready to walk out. She began removing her apron when the Sous-Chef put a hand on her shoulder to steady her. He was thinking of a big picture of his own.

"He'll write about us as well," he said to Dora. "If we do a good job, he'll write us all into the piece. We could use this."

Dora considered this.

"It's a win-win," Elza said. "But then I want you both to leave."

The Sous-Chef nodded. "I want one hundred thousand forints and a full week of pay for each of us."

"Fine," Elza said. Money was not the issue here. "I want everything prepared exactly as I say."

"Fine," the Sous-Chef said.

"And you?" Elza said to Dora.

Dora would have loved to have left the older woman in a bind, but she was smart enough to know that one hundred thousand and a full week's pay was a better deal than walking away empty-handed. So, she nodded. "Yes, boss," she said.

Elza turned to her line cooks and the Dishwasher.

"When they're gone, you'll get raises. But I want you to know that I'm not tolerating any more of your shiftiness or this mess in the kitchen. If you take a smoke break, close the door behind you. If you spill, clean it up. If you don't shape up, you'll be following them. Do you understand? Now I want this place cleaned up. Spotless."

The two line cooks looked at their feet. "Yes, boss,"

The Dishwasher laughed and his body shook. "A raise!" he said. "A raise!"

Then Elza went into the dining room and gave her waiters a dressing down. She made them straighten their ties and told them to polish the mirrors and their shoes. In one fell swoop, six weeks of summer madness had come to an end and she had regained control. She felt good when she went home that night. She took a shower and combed her hair. She slept peacefully. She did not run away in her dreams and she never once reached over for a companion who did not exist. The next day she went to the city thermal and treated herself to a hot bath and a massage. When she arrived at the restaurant that night, the kitchen was clean and her brigade was standing at attention. She cooked that evening for the first time in two years. She and the Sous-Chef prepared meals the way they had when she had first hired him. She called out for ingredients or side dishes and the Sous-Chef was ready for her, handed her whatever she needed. Once, their eyes locked, and Elza could not help but remember that this was how they had started their affair. On an evening like this, when they had just seemed in tune to one another. But those days were gone. She focused on the pans in front of her. Orders made it out in short time, and the customers who visited that evening told friends when they left how good the food had been, that the restaurant was certainly back on sure footing. Several customers asked for Elza to step out for their compliments, but she shook her head at the waiters and kept cooking. She was enjoying herself too much. She was too busy to waste time with all the mindless banter and idle chatting. She was too enthralled with what she was doing to waste time on playing gastronomic courtesan. Instead, she sent the Sous-Chef. He nodded appreciatively, put on a tall chef's hat, and made such haste to the dining room that he nearly tripped. He preened about the tables and thanked everyone as best he could with slaps on the back and handshakes. By God, this is how he would do it in his restaurant, he decided. He quietly told them about the bistro he was opening nearby.

"In a month or so," he said and looked over his shoulder lest Elza should stick her head out from behind the kitchen door. "Keep an eye open. My fiancée and I are opening it together. The Three Roses."

What news! The customers congratulated him. They ordered drinks and second helpings of dessert and toasted him as though it were an engagement party. The Sous-Chef beamed and told them all about his modern new bistro. It turned out to be a beautifully satisfying night for everyone at Tulip. One of the best they all could remember.

Six

As for this critic . . . on his end, the elusive critic could not have been more annoyed or unimpressed with the pair of men who had spent the past six weeks hounding him across Europe. Hounding him! And during what was the darkest period of his life.

While, in previous times, he might have disposed of them sooner—without hesitation or kindness—he was presently struck with a series of devastating events that were humbling him considerably. These events had been gut-wrenching and had stirred in him despair and foulness that he doubted he could ever recover from. Indeed, he was shaken to the core of his being and to the foundation of his personality. He had arrived at an abyss at which he began to take serious stock of his life and to question every major choice he had made thus far. He even questioned the merit and relevance of his beloved career: Was criticizing restaurants really an aesthetic undertaking as he had made it out to be over the past fifteen years? Or was it only a mask that served to cover his gluttony and need for self-aggrandizement, the result of a humble upbringing and low self-esteem?

Because this was the conclusion *he* was reaching. Furthermore, maybe what mattered most of all was not being critical, but being kind and generous to others. This would, of course, be very hard to manage. But if he didn't, then what? Who would care about him when he was dead? Who would come to his funeral? Because, with recent events, funerals were much on his mind.

What absolutely did not matter at this time, what could have hardly mattered less, were two odd men incessantly calling him, trying to entice him with the goings-on of some obscure restaurant and its aspirational chef. *Well, to hell with aspirational chefs!* he thought. *To hell with aspirations! It's all just sickness. Hazy mirages on the horizon. To hell with all of it!*

Now, the Critic wasn't interested in becoming a philosopher, per se, but he resolved to seek loftier truths, to be a kinder and more generous soul. The incident that set him off on his soul-searching and career-questioning was the death of his long-time companion, his true beloved, a tangled and overweight spaniel bitch named Isabelle, who had unexpectedly and violently died. She had been hit by a motor scooter on the Rue Saint-Denis in Paris when the pet sitter had taken her for a walk. The Critic was astounded that the pet sitter had walked his esteemed companion on such a seedy street, so far from their home near Père-Lachaise. He had been in Brussels at the time, on a trip to profile a restaurant, when he had received the frantic call. The Critic had packed his belongings, checked out of the hotel he had spent the night in, ridden a taxi to the train station, and boarded the next express train home. He informed his editor of the terrible news while riding in a first-class seat.

"My poor Isabelle," he had sobbed. "My darling Isabelle!"

The editor had looked up at a clock and wondered how long it would take to console his writer. He had always hated that dog. He had thought it a nasty and unhinged little creature. At best, it had been confused as to its status—had thought itself on equal footing with its human owner and the occasional visitor. At worst, it had been no better than a rabid rodent. The dog had slipped between episodes of megalomaniacal haughtiness and salivating palsy, and one could never predict which of the animal's personalities one would find at any particular time. Still, the editor had known of his writer's affection for the animal and had felt bad enough for his friend and tried to tell him something kind.

"Well, get home and see what can be done," he offered. "Don't worry about the restaurant profile. We'll reschedule. It'll be all right. Have courage! They can do a lot of things now with sick animals."

And, in fact, at that moment, Isabelle was being kept alive by her veterinarian, who was awaiting further instructions. The vet was well aware of the affection between dog and owner and offered the creature an array of painkillers to ease its suffering, if only a little. When the Critic arrived at the animal hospital only four hours after being called, carrying his valise and his hat in his hands, and his raincoat in the crook of his arm, the veterinarian met him at the door and escorted him to an examination room where Isabelle was . . . convalescing (as the doctor euphemistically put it).

But in reality, Isabelle's back had been broken. Her spine and cord were severed in two. Her hips were shattered. An X-ray showed that a lung had been punctured and was collapsing. Despite the painkillers, she suffered tremendous pain and was slowly drowning in her own blood. She lay on her side, panting, gurgling, and forlorn. When she heard the Critic calling out her name and saw him in the doorway, she grew hopeful and eager and, wanting to please him, she tried to unfold herself for him the way she had thousands of times over the past eight years. It was useless, of course. All she managed was to pathetically scratch the air in front of her, to crinkle the paper on the examination table, and to wet herself. The Critic's stomach sank at the sight of her. He felt instantly clammy and thought he tasted the morning's breakfast of two poached eggs, a kaiser roll and currant jam, and a cup of coffee rising from his gut. He quietly steeled himself for her benefit and dropped his things. He reached out to Isabelle and scratched her wet belly. He debated picking her up.

"She's suffering," the veterinarian said. "There's nothing more I can do for her. I'm sorry, but I suggest we euthanize her right away."

"She's suffering?" The Critic repeated the words and then turned on the veterinarian. He grabbed him by the lapel of his white coat. He was on the verge of smacking the man in the face. "Why did you allow her to suffer?"

The veterinarian's assistants grabbed the Critic and pulled him away.

"I thought you'd want to say good-bye," the vet said, pushing him off and arranging his lab coat. "I've injected her with painkillers, but it's not enough to make her comfortable."

The Critic buried his face in his hands. He sobbed. The assistants released him.

"Yes, yes," he said. "Of course. Of course. Thank you!"

He turned to his spaniel and rubbed her behind her ears. He crouched next to her and whispered at her.

"My love," he said and lost his voice a moment in a pathetic crack. He remembered taking her for walks along the Seine, to dog parks where she proudly refused the advances of mutts and humans alike. "My love, where did that sitter take you? Why were you walking along Saint-Denis like a common prostitute? Why did he take you there to be struck down among the filth and excrement of human existence? Why not a park? Or even the cemetery near home? What were you doing so far away?"

The Critic punched into his palm imagining the face of his pet sitter. Then he shook his head and kissed his beloved dog. He massaged her front paws. "Eight years we are together. Eight years and you are my most wonderful companion," he said. "Save for my dear mama, you have been the only other woman in this sad and empty life of mine . . . ."

Isabelle looked up at him with wet, doleful eyes. She scratched again at the air in front of her. She looked as though she also might weep. She didn't, however. She only sighed.

"I don't know how to continue without you, my love," he said. "You have brought me peace of mind. You warmed my heart. You saved me, Isabelle. You alone saved me from having an empty life."

The spaniel looked at the veterinarian and seemed to frown. The doctor motioned to his assistants and they left the Critic and his dog to be alone.

"I don't know how to go on."

Isabelle panted. She gurgled and scratched. She was begging to be picked up. The Critic nodded and hoisted her gingerly in his arms. He brought her to his face and kissed her head. He felt her soft fur, and he remembered how delicious it was to rub his fingers through it, how she trembled under his fingertips. He lifted her farther up until they were eye to eye and Isabelle licked him. Her small pink tongue flicked his lips. He returned her kiss. He was crying inconsolably now. Isabelle whined.

"I love you," he said—as if there were any doubt—and then he called out for the veterinarian.

When they finally euthanized the poor creature, the Critic sat beside her body and stroked her for a long time. The veterinarian and the assistants let him be for forty-five minutes. It was as long as they were able. They had a scheduled appointment coming in at the top of the hour, and so, finally, a pretty and petite receptionist, who had been hired for precisely this job, was sent in to coax the Critic out of the operating room with paperwork and a catalog of urns.

"We're so sorry for your loss," she said to him as she led him out by the arm. "These unexpected deaths are always painful. Luckily, we have a special package available that can alleviate your shock. For seven hundred Euros we can prepare Isabelle for you and place her remains in a handsome urn. You shouldn't have to live without her, and you won't! She'll always be there to answer your call. But the package ends in a week, so if you'd like it . . ."

The Critic waved his hand at her. He opened the catalog of urns.

"This one," he said straightaway. "The white porcelain with peacocks. She would have liked this. She liked to chase birds . . . and squirrels . . . and frogs . . . and sometimes little children."

"Yes, of course," the receptionist said. "Excellent taste. She'll be ready for pickup in several days. Of course, if you prefer, we can ship her to you."

The Critic shook his head and arranged to pick up the remains. Then he fled the animal hospital. He returned to his flat, but everything about it reminded him of Isabelle. There was her little red bowl in the kitchen. There was her heart-shaped pillow on the window seat. Her chew toy was on the sofa. He fell onto the sofa and held the toy. He gave it a squeeze and a sound came out. It wasn't a wheeze, but it also wasn't a whistle. It was both of those sounds. The last exhalation of a dying animal. A death rattle. The Critic threw the toy aside. He tapped his feet and looked around the flat. Now it was too quiet. He already missed the tinkling of her collar and her nails tapping against the parquet floor.

The critic felt as if he were lost, as if he were being tossed by waves. He did not know what to do with himself, but he couldn't relax. The phone rang. He didn't answer it. He knew it was those horrible men calling again. He stood up and walked out. He left to wander the city. He walked to the Gare de l'Est. He thought about buying the first ticket on the very next train available, but he didn't. Instead, he walked into a pub, and then he walked into a second, and then a third and a fourth. Eventually he looked up and was not surprised at all to find that he had made his way to Rue Saint-Denis.

It was late at night now on Saint-Denis, and he stumbled down the sidewalk peering into doorways. There was a long line of cars on the road, and pimps and women emerged from buildings and stuck their heads through the car windows. He shuffled slowly down the street looking into the faces of women until one, in particular, caught his eye. She was nearly exactly the same as the others in that she wore a leather bustier and a short skirt. She was different in that she also had a pointy face and had accessorized her uniform with a fur stole the same color as Isabelle. He stopped to look at it. He rubbed his fingers through it.

"Your name isn't Isabelle, by chance?" he asked.

She looked at him quizzically, saw he was drunk, and shrugged.

"Sure is, honey," she said. "That's strange. Do we know each other? Do you want to party?"

The Critic looked at the stole again and felt it had to be a message from *his* Isabelle. She was contacting him from the other side, maybe even possessing this woman. He took a closer look at the woman standing in front of him. She had the same doleful brown eyes as his Isabelle. He thought their wet noses shared a remarkable resemblance as well. He ignored the name on her gold necklace. She must have been borrowing it from someone. She turned away from him and walked through the threshold of a building. She turned again and beckoned at him to follow. The Critic rubbed his beard and followed after her and was met on the other side of the threshold by a tall man holding onto a leash that was tethered to a muscular and salivating terrier. This man held his hand up.

"What do you want?"

"I want Isabelle," the Critic said and motioned to the woman in the fur stole.

"You mean Michèle? She's one hundred fifty euros," the man said.

The Critic handed him a wad of cash and was given change. He was allowed to pass and he followed the stole into a courtyard and then into an apartment. He thought about what the fur would feel like on his cheek. He followed it through the apartment and into a bed chamber.

"Did my Isabelle send you?" he asked in a small voice.

"Uh-huh. She sure did, sweetie," the prostitute named Michèle replied. "She told me to give you whatever you want. You sure you're going to be able to perform in your condition?"

She took off the stole and threw it on a chair. The Critic followed it with his eyes, half expecting that it would run to him and scratch at his shins; but it remained still and lifeless where it lay. He walked to it and picked it up. He rubbed it against his cheek. It was only a knockoff fur, nothing like his Isabelle. But he held it in his hands anyway and turned toward the undressing woman.

"Do you mind if I hold this?" he asked.

"Kind of kinky," she said. "But suit yourself. Don't muss it up, though. It's my only one."

She started to unzip her top, but before she could get it all the way off, he sat at the foot of her bed and began telling her about his little spaniel, the real Isabelle, who howled sometimes. She listened as she let her top fall to the ground and she asked him if he was asking her to howl.

"Because stuff like that is extra," she said.

When he couldn't answer, she shrugged and said she would anyway. *Just this once.* But once he began reminiscing about his deceased companion, he began crying, and then he spilled his guts out to her, and soon enough—funny, he thought later, but it didn't seem to take much at all—he had her crying also, just as powerfully. And then she looked at him and said through her tears as she tugged on the zipper of his pants, "Isabelle was my grandmother's name! She died last week. She was always kind to me. The stole was hers."

The coincidence was too much for either of them. They rushed at each other, and she peeled his pants away in one furious movement. She began trying to wrestle him to her bed, but somehow only ended up tripping him, and he fell on top of her back. She was pinned underneath him, and save for her torso and head, she was enveloped by his body's mass.

The Critic closed his eyes, felt the fur stole in his hand, put his face in it, imagined it was the fur of his little spaniel, and breathed in deeply. He imagined Isabelle's beautiful gamey fur crushed underneath a motor scooter and, desperately wanting to save her, desperately wanting to save himself, he instinctively began to pump the idea of death out of existence. He pumped like a Great Dane. He squeezed the stole and pumped his pelvis until he found it hard to catch his breath, but even then, breathless, he pumped until, at last, the tiniest bit of puppy-eyed hope seeped out of him, until, at last, he exploded in gratitude on the haunches beneath him.

The Critic was gone for a second, maybe gone for two, but then he was right back. Only now he was smiling. Smiling because this woman beneath him, this kind and gentle and empathetic prostitute, knew just what he needed, and she was howling! This is exactly how he needed life to be, he thought. He'd made a connection! He had found someone to come to his funeral!

He felt better after this, and he offered her six hundred euros for the rest of the night. Then they howled and exploded over and over again until he understood what appreciation really was. In between sessions they cried, and at last they fell asleep clutching one another close.

A ringing mobile phone woke them early the next morning. It was his and when he answered he was surprised to hear his sister, Gina.

"Where are you?" she asked, and from her trembling voice it was clear she had also been crying. She must have somehow heard the news about Isabelle. They had certainly shared a few memories together—like the time they all went out for a walk around his arrondissement, where she had offered Isabelle a bit of buttered bread. "I called you at home all night."

"I'm at a friend's," he said and wished he hadn't. Gina knew of his predilection for prostitutes and disapproved of it. She told him so every chance she got. There was silence for a moment, during which he expected she would berate him. She did not, for there was a bigger issue at hand. His second crisis was about to begin.

"You have to come to Rome today," she said. "Mama is dead!"

The Critic stood up quickly, bouncing the ersatz Isabelle out of bed.

"What do you say?" he shouted. "What are you saying?"

"It's Mama," Gina said. "She had a stroke last night after dinner. We've been at the hospital all night."

The Critic shook his head in a state of confusion. It was impossible! He had only spoken to his mother a few days earlier. She had been fine. She had talked about visiting him later in the summer, had talked about him visiting the next Christmas. He had agreed and then he had promised not to work too hard. Dead? He mumbled incomprehensible sounds that scared the ersatz Isabelle. He fell to his knees and began bawling into his hands. His beloved dog! His beloved mama! Both gone in twenty-four hours. The Critic banged the floor with his feet. He screamed and threw a pillow.

Once she understood what was happening, the ersatz Isabelle desperately made haste in getting rid of this visitor before he had her role-playing something unseemly. While he cried and thrashed about on her floor, she got his socks and shoes on. She dressed him and then called a taxi and helped him in. She went along for the ride to the train station. She somehow pulled the destination out of him and bought the ticket he needed for Rome. She even waited on the platform with him and let him cry on her bosom. When it was time, they boarded the train and she got him to his seat and handed him a bottled water. She patted him on his head and told him to take care of himself. She let go of him and left him sitting on the train with tears in his eyes and under the nervous gaze of other passengers.

"His dog and his mama just died," she announced. "Someone please make sure he arrives in Rome."

The passengers nodded. The ersatz Isabelle returned to her apartment. She took off the gold necklace that read *Michèle*. She remembered that her grandmother, Isabelle, had worn glasses. She reached into a dresser and pulled out a pair of horn-rimmed frames. *What's in a name?* she asked herself. She should pay tribute, she thought.

When the Critic arrived to Rome, his sister, Gina, met him at the train station. Her face was steely, severe. When he approached her—before he could ask her what had happened, when he was reaching out to hold her, to give her a kiss, hoping to console her, trying to understand the details, before he could do any of that—she smacked him hard.

"God forbid!" she said. "You think I would kiss that smelly, fat mouth of yours? Who knows where it's been? While our mother is gasping her last breath in the hospital and calling out for you, asking where you are, asking to speak to you one last time, you're letting some trollop bounce around on your face! This is how you love us? Once we bury her I am done with you. Done! Understand? Come on now. We have to find the right sort of funeral parlor. We have a lot to do."

The Critic was devastated. He nodded and followed meekly behind her. He thought about explaining, but he could not. He followed Gina out of the train station and to her car. They visited seventeen funeral parlors that day. They took brochures and looked at 147 caskets.

Truth be told, the Critic's mama had not called out for him. She had not asked where he was. Rather, she had died quite suddenly at dinner, in between courses. She had just finished an appetizer of fried squid when her left temple had begun to buzz. She had tried to say something to her waiter about the squid's rubbery texture, but when she had looked up she had seen that her daughter Gina hadn't heard her and was staring back at her with that tortured look of concern she always wore on her face. Nothing to be concerned about, she had tried to say. Lighten up! It's only that the squid is rubbery. Only a bit rubbery.

And then her face had fallen into a bowl of tentacles.

Elza's instructors, well-meaning as they were, had harangued this unfortunate man with phone calls and messages while all of this was unfolding. When the old instructors couldn't reach him, they contacted the magazine's editor. The editor shook his head and didn't even bother explaining the situation to the men. *Oddly enough, there might be good to come of this,* he thought. A trip like this might be a good change of scenery for the Critic. It might give him something else to think about. The editor promised the instructors that he would speak about it with the Critic and that he would send him to Hungary as soon as he could.

Now, just returned from two funerals, one for his mama and a second for Isabelle—both lovely affairs with the appropriate amount of flowers, tears, and guilt—just back from quarrels with his sister, Gina, over property and prostitutes and years of recriminations, the Critic found himself roped into a visit he was not particularly keen on. He knew he was not himself. He was growing ever more erratic, ever more confused, ever more obsessed with the idea of his own funeral.

"I'm just vulnerable right now," he said. "It's not that I don't want to work." He did. He desperately wanted to work. He *had* finally reached the conclusion—while staying in Italy and fighting with his sister—that doubting life was only a form of self-absorption. It was a luxury. In thinking of his mama, he realized he hadn't grown up that way. She had had no patience for self-pity. It's why she'd left their father. He was always feeling sorry for himself. He had robbed a bakery with some friends after the war and had gotten caught—had, in fact, been the only one to be caught—when he had stopped mid-robbery to not only taste, but to eat, one cream pie, and then another, and then a third. He had not been able to stop! He was so sorry, he had told her afterward. Stupid, stupid, stupid, he had said through tears.

His mother had agreed with him and had left him to rot behind bars. And this is why the Critic wanted to work! He did. He couldn't allow himself to be held back. But he protested when the editor gave him his new assignment.

"I can't do this," he said to his editor. "Those people harassed me in my darkest hour. No empathy at all. As rapacious as vultures. The whole region, frankly. It's run amok. Always grabbing. And anyway, my specialty is haute cuisine! Fine dining. You should choose someone else for this sort of thing. I'm quite sure this is only peasant food! I haven't been a peasant since Mama remarried in fifty-eight."

"Look, just try it," the editor argued. "Just go and visit. We need to do something new. Think about the place for the Silver Ladle. It could be different. Exotic. We need to expand our readership. Subscriptions are slipping. Comments are coming in that things have become staid."

"Nonsense," the Critic said. "And I doubt that commenting on Eastern European fare is worth the paper. What do you need to know? Paprika probably. Onions. Sour cream. Peasant food, I tell you. There is no way that restaurant can be considered for the Silver Ladle, let alone for a profile."

But the editor insisted. He offered his friend an extended holiday around the country visiting wineries and eating meals. He offered him a tour around Budapest and a cruise up the Danube if only he would take some time off and visit—and eat at Tulip.

"They've invited you to a lake house for the summer. Take it!"

"What if I hate the place?" the Critic asked. "How will I be able to write a positive profile?"

"I'm only trying to convince you that it is worth your while to get away," the editor said. "See something different. Taste something different. You deserve a break. Visit their school. Visit the restaurant. Then take a holiday. Make friends."

It was that last bit that quieted the critic. Friends. People who come to your funeral! He considered the offer. *There might be something to it,* he thought. A clean slate where no one knew him. If he was mindful, empathetic, he might make a friend. It might be worth the trip. At the very least, he was so lonely at home without Isabelle he really did want to get away.

"Fine, the summer," he relented. "However, I must warn you that my profile might not be too flattering. You must understand that. Too much paprika is too much paprika, and there's no way around it."

"Yes, yes," his editor said. "You're absolutely right. But these people are persistent and have assured me a meal you won't soon forget."

"I've never forgotten a meal," the Critic said and rubbed his belly absentmindedly. "They're all right here."

Seven

Since she was ten, the most powerfully loaded word in Dora's house, in her vocabulary, had been *opportunity*. And from what little she knew or cared about history, it seemed to her that until 1989 the word, the concept, had not existed. Life *before* the change was all about cigarettes and salted bread rolls for breakfast, maybe a cup of cocoa in a milk house on the way to work or school. It was a dun-colored existence. If a person was ambitious, he or she joined the Party to get ahead, but most people kept their mouths shut and their heads down. They pursued hobbies like photography or tennis; or maybe they climbed mountains or kept a garden and traded whatever extra they had for something they didn't have; or maybe, if they were overly ambitious, they carried whatever extras they could round up to the co-op or the weekly market, and they sold it for a bit of change. Everybody was nearly the same—doctors, lawyers, garbage men—and for all of them, time had frozen in the year 1956 when Soviets had arrived in tanks. So there was no such thing as opportunity. Not really. Not until that wall fell, anyway. At least, this was history as Dora had heard it. She had still been a girl when the wall did come down, still in primary school, so she really could not have explained it to anyone one way or another. The only thing she had to go by was what her father told her. It was all history to her.

"Yours is a lucky generation," her father announced from his feet as they watched the television one evening and shook their heads at the graffitied wall collapsing hundreds of kilometers away. He hunched over and touched the screen as if he wanted to climb in and be transported to Berlin. He looked back at Dora and his wife. He paced the room like a zoo animal. A mischievous smile spread across his face. He was a man who had always been in some kind of trouble or other. He was the kind of man who sniffed out opportunities.

"I can't believe it! I can't believe it!" he announced to the room. "The future is wide open to us. We can go anywhere, do anything. Nothing can hold us back!"

Dora's family had been on an upswing ever since.

The very next day, Dora's father walked into the heating collective and announced to his fretting superiors that he could do a better job, faster, and that he didn't need their measly pay or their dilapidated timeshare in the mountains. He was going into business for himself, *thank you very much*. He'd buy his own cabin in the woods.

"What do you think you will do?" his superiors chortled. It was always the same with this guy. He thought he was smarter than everyone else. He was exactly the sort the system had been trying to do away with.

"I'll start my own business," Dora's father said. "I'll install and repair heating systems, water tanks, and boilers. I'll set up irrigation systems in the countryside. I'll do whatever I want!"

His superiors waved their hands at him, but he said good-bye to his friends. A couple of them asked him if they could go along, and he said sure. He had no idea how he would pay them, but he figured they would work it out.

That done and a heating business successfully started, he sold the family's summer garden near Lake Balaton to an Austrian for what was a considerable amount of money. He had a second idea, and with the capital, he bought an old shed in Delibab near the lake and university and he opened the city's first privately owned ice-cream stand. Once summer arrived and the continental heat was at full blast, the family made money at a brisk pace selling to all the people who went walking in the park—young lovers, young families.

"Who doesn't like ice cream?" he asked.

Dora and her mother worked the stand while her father expanded his boiler business. He indeed moved on to irrigation systems, and then in another twist, finally on to a government-divested potato-crisp factory on the outskirts of town. He was the only one in the area who could come up with the capital, and so he was the first—and, for a short while, the only—crisp maker in the country. The family sold their flat and moved to a refurbished villa after that. When an American crisp company came calling with an offer to buy in, Dora's father partnered with them and the family grew even wealthier. Dora and her mother still worked in the ice-cream stand for something to do. Making money was now in their blood. They were among Delibab's first homegrown capitalists.

In the ten short years since the changes, Dora's father had made enough money to live comfortably on for the rest of his life and for his children's grandchildren to live comfortably on for theirs—all of them able to pursue whatever interest they wanted as long as they could make money doing it.

"It was easy," he boasted when he was interviewed by a national weekly as a business leader of the new economy. Political parties sought him out for donations. The newly formed Lions Club asked him to be a charter member. "When I saw an opportunity, I took it. That's all anyone has to do. Not be afraid to take a chance."

Dora's family took the idea of capitalism and entrepreneurship so closely to heart that not much else was discussed or deemed important. They didn't attend the theater. They didn't listen to classical music. These were pragmatic business people, not intellectuals, and certainly not artists or sensitive to aesthetic natures. Yet, early on, they noticed little Dora had an artistic side. At the ice-cream stand whereas Dora's mother would scoop ice cream in a cone mechanically, Dora's cones were filled and decorated with care. They were painstakingly patterned with sprinkles or chocolate bits. Instead of reprimanding her, her mother let her do what she wanted. She called it a *Dora Special* and charged extra. Everyone was happy.

That was the most curious thing about this family. They were supportive and happy. They possessed no guile whatsoever. The whole point of their existence was to create wealth, and their whole secret to living was knowing that *anything* could create wealth. It was eventually decided, by everyone, that food, particularly desserts, seemed like a good path for Dora to take.

"It's creative and after you finish studying you could open a bakery or a café," her father said.

So she studied at the culinary institute in Budapest to become a pastry chef. There were no deviations along the way. They all agreed that once she finished her training, the potato-crisp family would expand their empire by opening their first dessert café in the centrum of Delibab. Then perhaps later, modifications could be made and prepackaged desserts could be frozen and boxed in the factory.

"A simple equation," her father exclaimed. "Produce cheap and simple goods and services that people want. Heating in winter, ice cream in summer, crisps all year round, and finally coffee and cakes. Opportunities, every single one!"

The only bump was encountered when Dora decided that while she did not mind opening a café, she might also want to own a restaurant. Her family initially balked at the idea: too much overhead. Plus, a restaurant's success was subject to a fickle public.

"Who'll manage the factory?" her father asked.

Dora and her mother looked at one another.

"I don't want to manage a factory," Dora said. "I want a restaurant."

Her father eventually relented. Dora had the family work ethic. She understood the purpose of work. He knew she'd give it a good go.

It was in this mind-set that she took on the duties of pastry chef at Tulip. It was obviously a profitable business, and Dora felt she could learn something by watching and working.

"It's a good model," her father agreed. "But it might be going out of style. Something to consider while you're working there. Crisps and ice cream never go out of style. Heat doesn't go out of style."

Dora nodded. She understood what he was saying, she really did, but she wanted a restaurant of her own and she knew Tulip was the best one in the city.

She had never intended to stay very long, just long enough to get a sense of how things worked. But as soon as she started, she was ready to quit. The way Elza worked—distractedly, at the time Dora arrived—was exactly the opposite of what she had learned at home. Dora was convinced that Elza's success was accidental, entirely based on luck.

Dora noticed how much waste Elza allowed in her business. Time was wasted. Money was wasted. She noticed that the Dishwasher's station was outdated and inefficient. She noticed that there were too many entrées on the menu. She also noticed that the best employees—the Sous-Chef and the Dishwasher—were not being used to their full potential, while the worst ones—those horrible line cooks—were given more consideration than they deserved. Dora saw that while Elza might have known how to cook, she didn't seem to know how to manage an organization.

"The Sous-Chef seems smart, though," she told her father. She reported nightly on the things she learned. "He's hard-working . . . and ambitious!"

Dora had developed a crush on the Sous-Chef almost immediately, and it was something neither she nor her parents had anticipated. She spoke about him all the time at home. She was confused, though, because she could not understand why he seemed so standoffish when she was hired, and she could not understand why Elza and he seemed to be fighting. He did his work well. There must have been something more.

Her desire to get his attention was the only reason she had stayed on at Tulip as long as she had. It was the only reason she put up with the foul-mouthed line cooks and the smelly old dishwasher.

It took a while for the Sous-Chef to notice her, but he finally did. It was the same night that Elza had refused his proposal for the last time and he had cleared out his things. That evening, the Sous-Chef went out drinking with friends. He complained about Elza and they shook their heads.

"She's an old lady," said one. "Like an aunt."

"Yeah," said another. "What are you going on about? She's doing you a favor. Fun is fun, but come on. You've been at her beck and call long enough. Why worry about an old saddle when there're girls like that lot there, sitting alone at bars and just waiting to be broken in?"

The Sous-Chef had followed their gaze in the direction of a

group of young women sitting at the bar, and staring pointedly back at him with her yellow curls and the evening version of her trademark smoky eyeshadow (it had glitter in it) were Dora and a few of her friends.

They had smiled at one another and waved and the two groups had quickly merged.

That evening was when the flirting had begun, and Dora was soon head over heels. The Sous-Chef was a bit slower, but he had to admit he liked her.

Wanting to be fully straight with her, though, he had told her about his relationship with Elza.

"No wonder!" she had said.

They talked, and she was impressed with his ambition. She invited him to her home for dinner one weekend, and the Sous-Chef accepted. To his credit, he liked the whole family immensely *before* he figured out who they were. But it took him all of twenty minutes to figure out that this wealthy family was *the* wealthy family. The famous crisp makers of Delibab. *How lucky to be sitting here,* he thought to himself.

"You're a smart man," Dora's father said. "What are your plans for the future?"

Nobody had ever asked the Sous-Chef that question before. He'd spent three years trying to share them with Elza, but she had never listened.

"Oh, I have plans," the Sous-chef said.

He looked in Dora's direction. Dora was sitting beside her mother at the table. He smiled for them. Mother and daughter both blushed. Dora's father glanced at his daughter and thought he saw a twinkle in her eye. He considered it for a moment.

"Everybody has plans, young man," Dora's father said. "What makes yours so special?"

"I've got more than plans," the Sous-Chef said confidently. He told Dora's father how he planned to sell his car, raid his savings, sell the weekend garden, and take a loan to make his own restaurant happen. This last part struck a chord. Dora's father looked the younger man over and offered him a second beer.

"It's a good plan!" he announced. "By God, selling the family garden is how I started. It's the beauty of opportunity. Ingenuity. The only thing holding anybody back anymore is laziness and lack of imagination. Son, if I could do it, then you can too."

The Sous-Chef beamed like a lighthouse. It had been a long time since a man had called him son. He thanked Dora's father and after dinner played cards with him. Dora came by later and pulled him away from the table. She wanted to go out to a club with friends.

It dawned on him that it had been at least three years since he'd gone clubbing. He had spent most of his evenings at the restaurant or trying to convince Elza to marry him. A little bit of fun was appealing and so he went.

When they were gone, Dora's mother sat next to her husband, who had grown quiet and was thinking deeply.

"I know what you're thinking," she said. "But she's still so young!"

"Bah! You were her age when we had her," he said.

"It was different then."

"It's an opportunity!" he announced, and he was the expert. "For her. For him. They like each other. They want the same things. It's a great opportunity. He's better than these skinny tattooed boys who are always hanging around . . . listening to loud music . . . no plans for their futures . . . no respect for the sacrifices that afforded them all the opportunities we never had . . . probably on drugs. I like him."

Dora's mother liked him too. She knew Dora did as well. She shrugged.

"If she'll have him," she said.

And Dora's father nodded and wished. He wished really hard that night when they went to bed. He wished and hoped and prayed that his daughter had the sense to grab an opportunity.

And of course she did! It was the family way. Dora and the Sous-Chef never made it to a club. As they left her house she brushed up next to him and looked into his eyes. He smiled at her. She was all glittery eye shadow and smelled of sugar and shampoo.

"Don't you want to take me somewhere?" she whispered.

The Sous-Chef thought about Elza. In all fairness, he did. In six seconds he thought about all the time he had invested in the relationship. He thought about how much he had learned from her and how generous she had been. He thought about all of it, really, but he also thought about how she had refused his proposals. Consistently. He thought about how many times she had said, no—as if he were asking her to go to the moon, as if he were being absurd. He thought about how she sometimes shrank away from him at night, how she seemed to want to escape from him. He wasn't a stupid man, the Sous-Chef. He knew his relationship with Elza was finished. And here, now, was someone else. The Sous-Chef looked at Dora and saw her in all her potential. Well, first he imagined her naked . . . but then, then he saw her potential! As a wife. As the mother of his children. As his business partner. He recognized the support system she came with. He saw it all, summed it up in another fifteen seconds. An opportunity like Dora *never* happens. A beautiful girl. A rich girl. Interested in *him*? Hell yes, he would take her somewhere!

"My sister is at her boyfriend's and my mother falls asleep at nine," he said. "Would you like to go back to my place? It's not as nice as yours, but my mother isn't a bother."

She agreed, and they stopped at a bar for a couple of drinks and to snuggle. At 8:47 P.M. he motioned for the door and they caught a taxi to his—and his mother's—home. They giggled as they stumbled in and his mother called from her bedroom.

"Who's there?"

"It's me, Mom," he said. "Me and a friend. Just go back to bed."

He took Dora to his room and they undressed. When his hands touched her he was surprised by how different she felt. She wasn't as soft as Elza, but she was definitely more energetic. They fell to his bed.

He figured they were engaged when he unbuttoned her jeans. He just felt it. But to be sure, as she was writhing and panting beneath him, as he cupped her bottom and kissed her throat, he moved up the side of her neck and whispered a proposal in her ear.

"God, yes!" she gasped.

The Sous-Chef was finally getting married!

Eight

Elza felt the brandy burn her throat, but she knew it would steady her nerves, and that would be useful to her now that her evening with the Critic had arrived. Last-minute preparations were taken care of: the mirrors had been dusted and polished, the linens were cleaned and pulled tightly over the tables. Both wash closets were in pristine working order. Elza personally examined each corner of the dining room and greeted her staff as they arrived. All the employees arrived in tip-top shape, freshly groomed and alert. The line cooks did not tarry, did not smoke, but instead started prepping ingredients in the kitchen straightaway. They diced onions and garlic; they prepared different cuts of pork and beef; they started a soup; they even began to mix the dill sauce called for in Elza's recipe.

She decided to open early for the Critic this night and had reserved one of the nicest seats in the dining room for him. The Critic's back would be to the kitchen doors and facing the great picture window. The view outside was softened with fresh bunches of tulips placed in vases along the windowsill. Tulips also stood in vases in the corners and on wall accents. The Headwaiter had arranged as many colors as Elza could find, and the flowers made the dining room warmer and more intimate.

Elza walked around the dining room and smoothed away invisible wrinkles on the tablecloths. When the Headwaiter arrived, she checked her watch. The Critic's train was ten minutes away. She'd have to leave now to meet him and her old instructors at the train station. She looked around the dining room one last time. She looked the Headwaiter over. When she was satisfied, she went into the kitchen to check on things there. She intended to meet the men at the train station and taxi with them immediately to the hotel across the street from her flat, where they could freshen up before dinner.

The Dishwasher arrived as she was inspecting the ranges. He patted her on the back good-naturedly.

"Big night, tonight," he said. "I can't believe it's here."

Elza could not believe as much either. It didn't seem possible that this would be happening to her. These kinds of things didn't happen here, she knew. In Paris, yes. Certainly in Berlin. Maybe occasionally in Budapest. But here? In little Delibab? Elza looked at her wristwatch again. Dora and the Sous-Chef were nowhere in sight. She knitted her brow.

"Nothing to worry about," the Dishwasher said, noticing she was beginning to breathe quickly. He was still patting her, settling her as though she were a skittish horse. "They're good kids. They'll be here."

"They're late," Elza said. She knew she sounded bitter. "I have to leave for the train station."

"Don't worry," the Dishwasher said. He ushered her to the kitchen doors and practically pushed her out. "I'll keep an eye on things back here. I'm sure they'll walk in any minute."

Elza smiled at him and returned an affectionate pat on the shoulder.

"I have to go," she said.

"So, go," he said and held the door open for her while pushing her a touch harder. "Go."

The sound of the line cooks working followed her through the dining room. One was whisking the dill sauce while the other prepared a leg of lamb. Despite the Dishwasher's assurances, Elza had a sinking feeling. She turned and stuck her head back through the kitchen doors.

"Get as much prepped as you can, would you?" she called out to the line cooks. "I'll need it all when I return."

The second line cook nodded and put down the leg of lamb. He headed to the refrigerator.

"You're going to be late," the Dishwasher reminded her and blocked her view.

Elza looked at her watch a third time and cursed. She left.

She caught an idling taxi at the corner and arrived speedily to the train station, only to discover that the Inter-City would be forty minutes late. The lady behind the glass at the ticket counter was surly and wouldn't give her any information. Elza thought she might begin hyperventilating at any moment. What was the point of planning anything, if the trains won't run on time? Elza rolled her eyes at the woman at the counter and walked over to a bench, where she sat. She called the restaurant from her mobile phone but there was no answer. Five minutes later, her mobile rang. It was the Sous-Chef calling her back.

"Where are you?" he asked.

"You made it!" she said.

"Of course I made it," he said. "We're both here. Dora's preparing the cake. The sauce is done and waiting. We had a problem with those kids tapping on the glass a minute ago, but the waiter sent them away and told them not to come back tonight. Otherwise, everything is picture perfect. The dining room looks great. Your regulars are arriving."

Elza smiled. This was good. She had extended an invitation to all her regulars—to Eva, to the Humanities Professor, the Postal Inspector, and the Motorcycle Officer. She had invited all of them. She wanted the restaurant to be lively. She wanted the dining room to buzz. She wanted to show the Critic that people actually ate at her restaurant. It was a place that *lived*. If there was any problem it was only that these people were supposed to begin arriving *after* the Critic had already begun his meal. She had wanted him to eat in peace, to get the full taste of her food before too many distractions came along.

"I guess that's fine," Elza said. "I'll bring him in as soon as I can."

"Sounds good," the Sous-Chef said. "Good luck, eh?"

Elza paused a moment wondering if she should respond. She recognized he was being tender. She decided to say the same in return, but a light flickered in the distance and caught her eye. Overhead, a loudspeaker crackled to life and announced the approaching train. People stood up and pointed. They began walking to meet it at its platform.

"It's here! It's here!" Elza said into her mobile. "Get started. We'll be there soon."

The train rattled and squeaked to the platform before the air brakes hissed and it lurched to a stop. Elza was standing, craning her neck down the line, trying to get a glimpse of her instructors. She caught a glimpse of herself in some glass and felt good about how she looked. She'd used a little mascara and a sensible amount of eye shadow.

She saw a hand toward the back of the train waving frantically and heard her name being called. It was all the way at the back, in the regular-fair cabins. She had offered to buy first-class tickets for them, but her instructors had refused.

"No need, no need," they had said. "It's our pleasure. We'll take care of it."

Now she wished she had made the reservations anyway. Elza hurried to the back of the train to meet them. The Professor of Sauces disembarked alone. Elza craned to see the Professor of Meats or the Critic behind him, but they weren't there. Something was wrong. The Professor of Sauce's eye looked bruised. He shook his head sadly at her. His hands were shaking.

"What is the matter?" Elza asked as her face fell into an approximation of his. She put her hands on his shoulders to steady him. "What happened to you? What has happened?"

It was clear the Professor of Sauces had been weeping. Elza took a tissue from her purse and handed it to him, but she kept craning her neck over the disembarking passengers. She handed the professor a second tissue. The disembarking passengers looked at her pityingly. She caught snippets of their conversation.

"What a nuisance," whispered a woman to her husband while staring pointedly at Elza.

"Disgraceful behavior," an old woman said to her daughters who had met her at the stairs.

"What is it?" she asked while pulling the Professor of Sauces away from the train to keep from blocking the other passengers.

"They tried to throw us off the train!"

"What?" Elza barely stopped herself from shrieking. "Who did? Who tried to throw you off the train?"

A chorus of singing voices from inside the train grew louder as their owners approached the open door. It was a group of rowdy men. Young, but clearly drunk. They were being followed by a conductor.

They reached the exit of the railcar and were stepping down when they spotted the Professor of Sauces.

"Hey! It's our little friend!" one of them shouted, and they all approached—six of them—tall, beefy young men with shellacked hair and smug faces. They were frivolous types, Elza thought—the kind who spent daytime hours in gyms and evenings at nightclubs.

"Hello!" one of them called out and sidled up next to her. "Who's this little birdie then? This your daughter, is it?"

The Professor of Sauces turned and scowled at them. He shook his umbrella.

"You! Keep away from us, you!"

The young man and his comrades laughed. He turned to Elza and smiled. It was a lascivious smile, as though they were presently in a discothèque and he had offered to buy her a large colorful drink, thinking she would then allow him to press his body against hers.

"Take it easy, princess," he said to the Professor of Sauces. All of the young men were looking at Elza now and smiling. The same dumb smile replicated six times. The same empty smugness. The train conductor standing behind them ordered them to walk on.

"What have you done?" Elza asked sternly in a flash of anger. "What have you done? Where are the others?"

The young men's faces changed again when they realized she was talking to them the way their mothers would. "We was just playing around!" the young man protested. "Honest! You tell her, princess. Tell her what you did. And I already told you to stop waving that damned umbrella at me."

The young man swatted the umbrella away and it fell to the ground. The other men laughed. The Professor of Sauces bent to pick it up and when the men made as if they might grab it, Elza took a step in between them. The train conductor moved between them as well.

"Where are the other two men who were travelling with this man?" she asked the crowd. "What have you done to them?"

"What? You mean that fat Italian and princess's boyfriend?" the young man said. "We haven't done anything. Anyway, we was just playing. A bunch of pansies, the lot of them. You'd think they'd know how to take a joke."

Elza saw the umbrella out of the corner of her eye. The Professor of Sauces had retrieved it from the ground and was swinging it. Elza tried to stop him, but the older man was too quick for her. Besides, he was swinging the umbrella for all he was worth, and Elza was afraid to take the blows.

As he swung, they started laughing and taunting him.

"They weren't really going to throw them off," the train conductor said as he tried to grab hold of the Professor of Sauces. "I think they were just having a laugh. The train stopped, see. Somewhere out in the countryside. They decided to have a party. They had some homemade brandy and they offered your friends a drink."

One of the young men pulled a soda bottle from his backpack. He shook it for Elza to see.

"Yeah," he said. "We offer them a little nip. Everyone's fine and happy and having a good time, except for princess's fat friend. We pass the bottle to him and he goes ballistic. A raving lunatic, that one. He starts shouting at us for no reason. Starts scolding us for having a good time. Calls us a bunch of peasant alcoholics and starts pouring our brandy out the window. He was pouring out our brandy, miss! Right out the window and then onto the floor of the train. The guy's a real mess. So I snatch the bottle away, and that's when he pushes me. Really. He pushes me. Well, you don't expect me to stand there and take that, do you? Not from a fat foreigner and a couple of pansies. I push him back, and then me and the fellas decide it'd be funny to teach him a lesson, and we make like we're going to throw him off . . . I don't know, maybe we would have, but then princess here starts swinging his umbrella and hits himself in the eye. They caused havoc on the train, miss. The lot of them. That's when the conductor came and everything went to shit. He *sent* those other two buggers to the dining car."

"I did, miss," the train conductor said. "I thought it'd be better to separate them."

"The dining car!" Elza's face fell at the thought of what they'd eaten as they sat and waited.

"It's right there, miss," the conductor said.

"I'm sorry for the misunderstanding," Elza said to him.

She grabbed the Professor of Sauces and ran to the dining car. They boarded and found the Professor of Meats and the Critic sitting on stools drinking beers.

"Elza," the Professor of Meats exclaimed and pointed at her. "We were just coming out. This is Elza!"

The Critic turned around. His face was blotchy and his eyes were red.

"You're the chef!" He grabbed Elza's hips. "The aspirational chef!" He spoke in English, assuming it would be the easiest.

"Pardon!" Elza said and took a step back. She could feel herself losing control. She wanted to deck him right in his nose. How dare he! She tried to refocus. "We have to get off this train. We've slowed it down enough. It's about to leave. We have to get off at once!"

She pulled the Professor of Meats, who pulled the Critic. They stepped off just as the train was pulling out.

"Aspirational chefs make me sick!" the Critic announced. "Do you know how many of you are out there? It's always the same. Always so damned desperate. Always so hurried. What's the point? You should take it easy, Miss Chef. What do you expect will happen? What do you think you'll achieve?"

Elza didn't respond. She was wondering the same things herself. She took his hand and shook it. "Elza Molnar," she said firmly and sternly.

The Critic let out a boozy sigh. Elza turned her face away in disgust.

"Too much paprika is too much paprika," he laughed.

"Sorry, Elza," the Professor of Meats said. "Getting him drunk was the only way to calm him down. His mother died recently. And a dog, I think. He's just back from their funerals. I had no idea. I think that's what he said. My English isn't what it used to be."

Elza said nothing. She led the lot to the taxi stand and then the hotel. As she waited in the lobby, the professors escorted the Critic upstairs to his room. They returned a few short minutes later.

"He says it's too noisy," the Professor of Sauces announced. Elza could tell that he was equally tired of the whole affair. "They're renovating the floor. Putting in air conditioners."

A second room was offered, but was also found unacceptable. A third was offered, and then a fourth. The sixth room was the one the Critic finally accepted. Elza was fuming at this point. She sat in the lobby and called the restaurant.

"Where are you?" The Sous-Chef picked the telephone up quickly this time. "We have a problem here with the meat. It's not going to be possible to—"

"No," Elza shouted to cut him off. Heads in the lobby turned in her direction. She smiled and lowered her voice. "No problems! We have a deal. You're not allowed to have any problems. Whatever it is, fix it."

"Well, it's just that—"

"Fix it! We have a deal."

"Fine," the Sous-Chef said angrily and hung up.

The Critic and the Professor of Meats came downstairs. The

Critic's face was less blotchy. He had tried to clean up. He presented his hand to Elza.

"Pleased to meet you," he said in a clearer voice than he'd had at the train station. A change had occurred in him. He was a lot less drunk and a bit more gracious. He looked more like the version she'd seen of him in the magazine. "Sorry about before. I had too much. Anyway, you're quite lovely and I am excited to see about your restaurant."

Elza looked at him and then at the professors. *This man is insane,* she thought. *At the very least, he is unhinged.* She recognized it instantly, and she wondered if he recognized it in her. She was already drained from the evening and it hadn't even begun. She smiled at him anyway. Empathy, she reminded herself. Enthusiasm.

"Well, then. Are you hungry?" she tilted her head and smiled. Her eyelashes fluttered.

The Critic's Adam's apple hopped in place. He nodded.

"Famished," he said.

They walked out of the hotel onto the promenade and headed for Tulip. Elza spotted the boys from the neighborhood, who spotted her as well, and she tensed as they ran in her direction.

"Hey, restaurant lady!" the tallest one called. "What are you doing at the hotel? Where are you going? We were at the restaurant earlier. Look at Pisti's new dance."

The one named Pisti began twirling and shaking his feet. The other two began to clap and sing. Elza and her group kept walking. The professors tried to shoo them away.

"Run along now," Elza said and smiled at them. "Go on. Run along."

The boys looked up at the Critic.

"Wow! What a fat man!" they shouted. "Hey, restaurant lady. Who's the fat man? Is he a foreigner? Will he give us money? He watched Pisti dance."

Elza was embarrassed, but she was glad they were speaking Hungarian. "Run along," she said again. "Please."

"But is he a foreigner?"

"Yes," said Elza. "Now run along."

But instead of running along, they ran alongside. The professors continued to try to shoo them away, but the boys were too fast for the old men. They put on pathetic-looking faces and grabbed the Critic's hand. They brought their hands to their mouths and bellies.

"Money. Dollar. Euro. Please. Money."

The Critic shook them away like cobwebs stuck to his skin. "I don't have any," he said. "Go on, get away."

The children hesitated. They looked at him again and then back at Elza.

"What a stupid fat foreigner," they said.

"Please run along. There's nothing here for you. Please," Elza said.

"Oh, restaurant lady! Why are you walking with this fat man? You're acting like a stinky witch!"

"Yes, Yes," Elza said. "That's right. I'm a horribly stinky witch and if you don't run along now, I'm going to cook you and feed you to him."

She said it viciously—so viciously that the boys fell back startled. They muttered under their breaths and took off down the promenade.

Nine

Two hours later than had been planned, the weary group of people arrived at Tulip's door. After a cursory look around the establishment, the Critic slumped down into a chair and Elza requested that a cup of coffee be brought immediately. She thought she might need to perk him up, awaken his senses.

When the coffee arrived, he looked at it and roared. "What is this?"

Elza looked at the cup of coffee to see what the matter was.

"It's coffee," she said. "I thought you might want a cup. It's been such a long day."

As she feared, she had insulted him.

"What?" the Critic shouted. He'd forgotten all about his resolution to be generous and kind. "You doubt my palate? I've eaten and drunk at restaurants ten times better than this one, and the chefs there were happy to have me, miss. I'll have you know that I am no amateur. This tongue is not an amateur's."

The other customers in the restaurant—who had been sitting there for more than an hour—were aghast at the shouting foreigner. They couldn't quite make out what he was saying, but they felt sorry for Elza. They wondered at how poised she managed to appear . . . but also how *meek*. Nothing was worth that type of abuse, half of them thought. The Motorcycle Officer and the Postal Inspector were about to stand up and say something, to throw the man out, even, but Elza spotted them and discreetly shook her head. She remembered the warning her professors had offered. *A ruffian. A lout. A bully.*

"The entrée tonight is special," she proceeded with a smile. "It's the latest addition to our menu. I would love for you to try it. It's a pork tenderloin in a paprika-dill sauce. Traditional ingredients. Locally produced."

The Critic closed his mouth and cocked his head. He loved pork! He nodded.

"Now that sounds like something I could sink my teeth into," he said a little less gruffly. "How do you say you prepare it?"

"Well, we use dill and sour cream. We bread the pork and sear it. Fresh potato dumplings come alongside." Elza motioned to the Headwaiter, who ran back to place the order.

"Sounds interesting. Very promising. Simple, but very promising. How do you prepare the pork?"

"A white wine marinade," Elza said. "Very tender, very pungent. I think you'll enjoy it."

The professors nodded from the next table.

"A very good dish, sir," said the Professor of Sauces.

"Salad?" the Critic asked.

"A simple cucumber salad," Elza answered. "Something light and clean for the tongue."

"Dessert?"

"A cottage cheese soufflé topped with a fresh, house-made red-currant sauce."

The Critic smiled again. She noticed he was already twisting his napkin. Elza smiled, too.

"All good choices," he said. "Very well, bring me a menu. I'd like to choose my own appetizer. But I must say I'm intrigued by your dill pork, aspirational chef. I'm intrigued!"

Elza nodded and took him the menu; she had translated it especially for the occasion. He examined it carefully and then he set it down in front of him.

"There," he said. "This one. The bacon and seared goose liver over fried cornmeal. I'd like to try that, if you don't mind. It sounds promising, and I don't believe I've tasted that combination before."

"It's very hearty," Elza said. She thought about the chef in Barcelona and smiled to herself. He was an erratic man, this critic, but a peasant at heart. She left him and carried the order to the Sous-Chef herself.

The Sous-Chef nodded when he received the order. Elza thought about explaining what had taken them so long, but looking at the Sous-Chef only made her angry. She watched as he seared a thin strip of goose liver along with a strip of bacon. The line cooks stopped what they were doing in order to prepare the cornmeal. They used a mold to create a small puck-shaped portion of polenta from the batch they had cooled and covered. After browning the puck on both sides, they passed it on to the Sous-chef, who arranged the glistening liver and bacon over the top of it and then crumbled a small bit of goat cheese on top of that. The Headwaiter collected the dish and presented it to the Critic.

Elza stepped into the dining room again. Everyone was eating and talking. It seemed as if everyone was enjoying themselves. Elza wished she could enjoy herself as well. In fact, she couldn't wait for the evening to end. She would go home, shower, and go right to sleep.

She watched the Critic as he cut into the liver and bacon and placed the pieces along with some corn meal onto his fork. He put it in his mouth and nodded. He was pawing his napkin, running his fingers along it. She waited until he twisted it and then she went back to the kitchen and took over from the Sous-Chef, who was already searing the pork for the entrée. One of the line cooks was cooking dumplings in a pan. The air in the kitchen smelled delicious, Elza had to admit it. She let herself feel hopeful. The kitchen was buzzing with activity from all the other orders coming and going. It had turned into a full night.

"It should be ready soon," the Sous-Chef said. "What's he like?"

Elza shook her head. "He is terrible. Horrible. Worse than I imagined. Completely erratic, and probably a manic depressive."

"Well, one taste of this should set him straight," the Sous-Chef said.

Elza looked at Dora. "How's the dessert?"

Dora pouted. She did not like the fact that the former lovers were standing so close to one another and having a conversation. She pretended not to hear.

"Dora," Elza said. "How is the dessert?"

"My desserts are excellent," Dora said in a clipped manner. "You know, we're engaged. This is the last night you'll see him."

Elza looked up at Dora. Dora was looking at the Sous-Chef. Elza looked back at the Sous-Chef, and the Sous-Chef blushed.

"It's true," he said.

It had gone that far so quickly?

"That's wonderful!" she mustered, and turned away. "Do you have the salad?" she asked the line cook.

It is finished, Elza thought. *All of it is finished. The Sous-Chef will leave, Dora will leave. I can begin again, and in an hour all of this will be a memory.* She was thankful she had survived.

The pork loin finished cooking and the dill sauce was added and it was arranged on the plate with the dumplings. They would serve the entrée together with the salad, as was their custom. She handed the plates to the Headwaiter, and he carried them out to the dining room. The Sous-Chef followed Elza to the door.

"Elza, about the pork, there's something you should know."

One of the line cooks looked up from his station.

Elza stopped and turned around. "Tell me later," she said. "Really. Not now. I don't think I could take one more thing. This evening has been a nightmare already."

The Sous-Chef shook his head. She never let him talk! In the three years they were together she was always shushing him. He threw a dish towel on the counter. He looked at Dora. Elza walked out.

The candle on the Critic's table flickered as he breathed over it. He had finished his goose liver. The Headwaiter had given him a glass of dry red and he was sipping from that. He was quiet at least, Elza thought, patiently awaiting the next course. Elza and the Headwaiter approached him. Figuring that at this point, with everything that had gone on this evening, they were past decorum, she sat across the table from him. She smiled. The waiter placed his food in front of him.

"Aspirational chef," he said. He seemed in a good mood now. "The goose liver was delicious. I've never tasted it quite like that before. Cornmeal. Who ever heard of such a thing? Quite a good idea. It was really very good."

He looked down at his food and smiled. "What a lovely presentation!"

He took his hands away from the napkin on his lap. He took up his table cutlery. He cut a dumpling in two and ran it through the sauce. He put it in his mouth and chewed. He picked up his napkin and dabbed his mouth. He twisted it before it went back on his lap. Elza's heart quickened. He liked it!

"Good," he said. "Tasty sauce."

"Thank you," she said.

He polished off the dumplings and then sipped his wine. He motioned to the glass.

"Really quite excellent. Is this a local?"

Elza nodded. "Yes, from the same region as our Tokaj vineyards. Not too far from here."

The Critic smiled before slicing the pork and putting a bite in his mouth. He took a couple of quick chews and then his face fell. His head tilted quizzically. Elza mirrored his movements until she heard someone else in the dining room gasping.

"Are those the same children from the hotel?" he asked and pointed with his fork. "What on earth are those boys doing?"

Elza turned to look behind her and standing at the window were the three boys. They had returned. They had taken their shirts off. It took Elza a moment to catch her breath. Not now, she thought.

"Hey, fat man!" the boys sang and pressed themselves against the windowpane. A few customers tittered.

"You're so fat," they called to him. "You're so fat and we're so hungry. See! We're so skinny!"

They held their stomachs.

"Hungry," they said.

The Critic knitted his eyebrows. Elza looked at the Headwaiter, who left the dining room to chase them away.

"Money," they called out. "Give us money. Euros."

"You must leave," said the Headwaiter sternly. "Leave right now or I'll call the police on you. Today is not the day for this."

"But we're hungry," they said. "And he's so fat."

"You're not hungry," the Headwaiter said. "Do I look stupid to you? Go away this instant."

The Critic put his knife and fork down and pushed his plate away. He watched the whole thing from his seat. He looked at Elza and shook his head. He pulled a notebook out of his breast pocket and jotted a few notes.

"What are they saying?" he asked.

Elza shook her head. "They're only begging for money," she said. "Take no notice."

"I can't concentrate," he said. "The appetizer was excellent and the sauce is delicious, but I can't work like this."

"They'll leave in a moment," Elza could hear herself begging. She could not believe that after everything that had occurred, it might all unravel because of those boys.

The tallest boy pressed himself against the glass. Giving up looking hungry, he had produced a bag of cherries, shoving handfuls into his mouth. Juice stained his palms and fingertips. It seeped out from between his lips and dribbled down the sides of his chin. From there, it fell to his sternum and grew like a beesting.

He peered into the restaurant, leered into it, and opened his mouth in a laugh. Bits of cherry and stones fell out, which made him laugh more. The Headwaiter tried to pull him away from the window, but he couldn't budge him without hurting him. The other two boys egged him on. The boy began licking the glass. He licked the glass and moaned; patrons that had been trying to ignore him put down their menus to watch uncomfortably.

The Motorcycle Officer looked at the Postal Inspector.

"This won't do Elza a bit of good," he said.

He grabbed the napkin from his lap and tossed it angrily onto the table. He stood up and made his way to the window. When the boys saw him approaching they shouted and darted away like frightened finches. They vanished into the shadows. He returned to his seat. Elza had to admit to herself that she was glad he was there.

"I am sorry," the Officer said to the Critic in halting English. "You know we have these Gypsies here."

The Critic nodded and thought about the gravediggers who had lowered his mother's casket in Rome. He felt suddenly teary-eyed. He focused on his plate. He sliced a second, larger piece of meat and put it in his mouth.

"This is tender," he said. "Very good. Very good."

Elza smiled. The critic chewed and chewed, but then he looked at her quizzically again and Elza instinctively looked behind her to see if the boys had returned.

"What?" she asked. "What is it now?"

"You said this was marinated in white wine?" the Critic said. "I was interested in seeing how the taste mixed with the cream and dill."

"It is," Elza said. "A white wine marinade that I prepared myself."

The Critic shook his head.

"My dear, this meat is only brined," he said. "A simple brine. Don't get me wrong, it's good. Just nothing special. The goose liver over cornmeal—that was original. And this dill sauce is very good also. But this entrée is only edible. It isn't extraordinary."

Elza felt as if she had been physically pushed down into her chair. She blinked and tried to catch her breath. She tried to say something, but nothing came out of her open mouth. The Critic continued eating. She watched how he would occasionally stop and twist his napkin in delight. He liked it. She knew he liked it. Why couldn't he say he liked it?

"Very good, though," he said. "The sauce is excellent. Still, it's only a pork chop."

She saw the Sous-Chef peeking from behind the kitchen door. She excused herself to go to the kitchen.

"Elza," he tried to whisper as she approached. "Let me explain. I can explain."

"You," she growled and grabbed his hat from his head. She swung it at him several times. He put his hands up to defend himself. "You did this on purpose! You're a saboteur!"

He fell back, fell back to Dora's station, and as he did, his elbow hit the Critic's dessert. The red-currant soufflé crashed to the floor. Everyone in the kitchen stopped what they were doing and looked at it. The Dishwasher came out, the line cooks, Dora, even the Sous-Chef and Elza stopped.

"Shit," the line cook said.

"That's bad," the Dishwasher said.

"Elza, the pork. We were late. Those people you invited came earlier than they were supposed to. Those idiots served it," the Sous-Chef said and pointed at the line cooks. "When we arrived we had to prepare something quickly. It was the only way. Honestly."

"Hey," the nasty line cook came from behind his station. He approached the Sous-Chef. "It's not our fault! Nobody was here to tell us what to do. There wasn't a sign on it. Everybody wanted pork tonight."

"Get out," Elza shouted at the Sous-Chef. "Get out! Get out! Get out!"

Dora left first. She was the first one to storm through the dining room. *Let her pick up her own mess,* she thought. She was glad to be done. The Sous-Chef, on the other hand, hesitated; he continued to try to explain it, but when he understood that Elza would never listen to him, he finally gave up. He decided a clean break was probably best. He ran after Dora.

Elza found herself facing the line cooks, on the verge of tears.

She dabbed her eyes with a dish towel and gave out a shuddering sigh. The men stood uncomfortably still while she composed herself. When she had done what she could, she turned to head back to the dining room.

"I didn't realize either," the Dishwasher called out. "Elza, my dear, I am so sorry."

"Is everything all right?" the Critic asked when she sat down again. He kept looking behind him toward the kitchen. Elza noted that he had cleaned his plate.

"What was the shouting? Who were those chefs who just left?"

"I fired them."

The Critic considered this. He felt sorry for this woman. For all of their sakes, it was time to end this game.

"I'm not sure what has happened here tonight," he said, "and though the food is good, you must realize that this is not really haute cuisine. I don't see how I could give you much of a review. This isn't the sort of thing we cover. Don't get me wrong, it's very tasty. Traditional and folksy. It's a great restaurant. But this is simple food like my mother might have made before she passed away. Would you mind if I skipped dessert and returned to the hotel? I'm suddenly very tired."

Elza just nodded, exhausted herself.

The Critic stood up and the professors did also. Elza stood up, and the Critic put his hand on her shoulders. They all walked to the door.

"Not every restaurant needs to be famous," he said. "What's the point of that? Your food was good. I enjoyed it. You seem to have lots of customers. Isn't that enough? You've read my column, I take it. I couldn't put this in my column. I couldn't recommend this for the Silver Ladle. I'm sorry."

The air was warm. Elza thought she should say something, but she didn't know what. Her professors seemed so disappointed. They had worked so hard. They had endured so much this evening.

"Hey fatso!" the three little boys appeared again out of the shadows. "Money. Please. Money. You're so fat. We're so skinny!"

"This is a madhouse!" the Critic said. "I'm really very sorry. I have to go and rest."

The professors hailed a cab and the three men tried to get in. The children crowded around the doors and pushed their hands at the men.

"Go away," Elza shouted at them and pulled them away from the taxi. They were like bees circling a flower.

"Good night, dearie," the professors called out to her from the taxi window. "We'll call you in the morning before we head out."

"Fatso! Money. Please."

The taxi sped off. The children chased the car a few meters, until it turned the corner and went away. They laughed and giggled as if they were celebrating something. They returned to Elza, who was still standing there. Who had not moved.

"Hey, restaurant lady," they said. "Was that foreigner mean to you? He was a fatso. Can you give us something? You're not really a smelly witch. Please?"

It was as if she didn't see them. They waved their hands in front of her, but she didn't respond. The eldest boy grabbed her and yanked her arm. Elza snorted. It was too much. Just too much. She was embarrassed. Her dream was gone. Her chefs were gone. She didn't know how to carry on.

"Please, restaurant lady. Some money. Or maybe some food." The boy was yanking her arm hard. The others waved their hands in her face to get her attention.

"Get away from me!" she shouted, shoving the smallest of the boys, and then swung her arm wildly.

She swung it hard, with all the anger of the evening bubbling inside her. The tall boy it was heading toward saw the flash of white and ducked. He looked up at it and it sailed over him like the swooping wing of a bird. Crouched down, he followed it with his eyes and saw it connect against the face of his smaller cousin, Pisti, the same one Elza had shoved—the one whose instincts, wrongly, told him to lean back instead of duck. When Elza's hand hit him, he lost his balance completely. He turned his body as he fell, but he didn't manage to get his hands out in front of him. He fell face first against the street curb.

For a second, after she had swung and they had finally let go, Elza felt better; but the feeling lasted for only a second—maybe half—because then she heard the sound of a wet drum, a thud, the crunch of bone hitting against pavement. Her stomach turned. She thought she heard her customers inside the restaurant gasp. She had suddenly returned to herself and was keenly aware of what had happened.

"I'm so sorry," she said and hurried to the fallen child. The Motorcycle Officer and the Postal Inspector were already at the door.

Several pedestrians stopped. They'd heard the gruesome noise as well

"What are you doing?" a woman asked her.

Elza looked at them while kneeling beside the groggy child.

"It was an accident," she said. "I didn't mean to. They were yanking my arm and waving their hands in my face. I swatted wildly."

She turned the boy over. Blood covered his face. He was moaning and dazed. The pedestrians gasped at the sight of the blood.

Elza held the boy steady by his shoulder and reached into her pocket to get a tissue. As she started to wipe the boy's face the other boys pushed her. She fell away from the injured one, and in that brief moment, before the Motorcycle Officer could get a hand on them, the healthy boys pulled the injured one to his feet and pulled him away as quickly as he was able to move. They half-dragged him down the street.

"Hey, come back," the Motorcycle Officer shouted.

"You have to go to the hospital," a pedestrian shouted after them.

One of the healthy boys turned his head and let loose a string of curses while gesturing at them. The pedestrians muttered their disapproval. The Motorcycle Officer gave chase for a few steps, but the boys ran into traffic to cross the street, the healthy ones pulling the little one all the while. He was stumbling like a drunk. Then they vanished behind a stream of cars.

"Come back!" Elza was standing. She took a few steps in the same direction as the boys, but she was glad they were leaving. She was glad! She was glad the officer was not giving chase too lustily. He took a few steps in their direction, but gave up rather quickly when he realized they intended to vanish. She held her breath and wished they would run away faster. Disappear from sight entirely. Melt back into whatever shadow they had emerged from.

"Come back!"

The pedestrians fretted and clucked like so many loose hens.

The Motorcycle Officer returned. He was winded. His belly rose and fell in front of him. He shrugged. Elza waved her hands as though she were trying to push away a bad smell.

"You see?" Elza said to the pedestrians. "They ran off! They seem fine. They are fine, I'm sure. We'll see them tomorrow."

"Gypsies," the Motorcycle Officer stated flatly to the burgeoning crowd and went back inside the restaurant to finish eating. "I wouldn't make too much out of it. It's certainly not worth a report."

Elza could have kissed him for that.

The pedestrians considered this. They looked down the street, but the boys were completely out of sight. They looked through the restaurant window at the Motorcycle Officer and the Postal Inspector. The two men had resumed eating and seemed entirely calm. The pedestrians milled about a little longer, unsure of what to do.

"Gypsies or not," an elderly woman scolded Elza, "you should know to be more careful with children. Treat them like you'd want strangers to treat your own. What if someone did the same to yours?"

Elza nodded. "Of course. Of course."

"Unbelievable behavior. Inexcusable."

Elza agreed. "It was an accident. A horrible accident. But you see, they're fine."

"That sort of thing makes us look bad," another pedestrian said. "There are tourists walking about, you know. You can't go around slugging children. This is Europe now, after all!"

Still, it was clear that there was nothing left for them to do. They finally walked away, muttering under their breaths and turning occasionally to look back. Elza's face felt hot. She was embarrassed and also sorry for the child. She *was* relieved they had run off, though. She'd give them some food if they came by tomorrow. Maybe some money. Maybe even offer them a little job helping in the restaurant. Something to show that there were no hard feelings, that it had really only been an accident. She'd say something to the flower girl if she saw her later. She walked back inside, past the reproachful eyes of her customers. She wondered how she would save everything she had from collapsing around her.

Book Two

Ten

It was not the first time the boys had made their way home injured. Over the years since they had first been let out to roam—to walk unaccompanied to the train station to scrounge for money or to stow away on trams looking for fallen change—they had suffered a multitude of accidents around Delibab. In fact, there had been countless forgotten scrapes and bruises, and countless tufts of hair and pieces of skin had been left behind in sacrifice in the various corners of the city. And despite their short lives, the boys had each managed to collect two or three incidents that were really worthy of discussion, worthy of repeating back in their quarter. They wore their collected injuries like medals, pointed at them when they met other children as a way to establish their toughness and dominance.

For example, one of the stories the eldest boy liked to repeat came from a time several years back when a professional circus had set up on the outskirts of the city behind the Polish market—where counterfeit items were sold and money was exchanged—and the boys had snuck in to see it. The circus was a wholly professional concern, a state-subsidized undertaking from the West, complete with dancing elephants, juggling Ethiopians, and churlish clowns who marched about, who didn't juggle or pull streaming multicolored handkerchiefs from their orifices but who seemed contemptuous of the whole affair, who behaved as though they were insulted at having to perform in the flatlands of Europe. Still, it was completely unlike any dusty, slapdash circus the boys had seen up until that point, completely unlike the only other circus they had been to, which had housed a mangy, toothless brown bear that had only lumbered through hoops when it was kicked.

There were tall vinyl tents that remained white and clean for the two weeks that it stood, as though a magical kingdom had materialized on the plains. The tents were heated at night! There was recorded music and generators. Even security. The boys had never seen so much security before—men with short haircuts, walkie-talkies, and sunglasses. Men who patrolled the grounds looking for trouble, looking for children like them, who spoke in multiple languages and were built like prizefighters.

"So many of them," the eldest boy wondered as he counted the security guards and cased the big top. "Look how many! More of them than elephants."

But the boys were not put off. They walked the perimeter of the circus grounds twice scanning for a point of entry. It took them thirty minutes to come up with a plan, but at last they found a quiet spot near the animal cages and took turns digging a hole under the fence. When they broke in, the fronts of their shirts and their faces were filthy with dirt, but they made their way triumphantly to the main tent just in time for the acrobatics show.

They only managed to steal all of fifteen seconds watching the acrobats, but what seconds! In the time they managed before a security guard noticed that they weren't wearing plastic bracelets, the boys were transported, imagining *themselves* as circus acrobats. Twirling and spinning through the air in flashy costumes with no net beneath them. They were rapturous. And they beamed as they imagined audiences across the world watching them fly above their heads with mouths dropped open. Their faces flushed when they heard the thunderous applause. Even when the security guard had called for assistance and four grown men had surrounded them and led them out of the tent by their ears, the boys strained their necks and stretched their earlobes to watch, to steal another second or two. When they were booted from the circus grounds entirely, they still felt they had won. They had seen something magical.

They left the circus behind and passed over the bridge back into the city. The eldest hopped onto the railing as though it were a tightrope. He stood on one foot. He twirled.

"This is how we'll do it," he explained to his cousins.

The other two nodded and clapped for him. They oohed and aahed for him, and he did a somersault on the railing. He did it once. He did it twice. He stood up and bowed.

"Do it again! Show us again!" the boys called out.

He puffed out his chest and attempted a third somersault, only this time he fell. He tumbled off the rail—and though he was lucky to fall onto the bridge instead of down into the railyard, he landed with a crunch.

"What was that sound?" His cousins squatted beside him.

"My arm!"

But it was still a memorable day. And well worth a broken arm. As he walked home crying and holding his arm out to his side trying not to shake it too much, his cousins tried to make him feel better by talking about the circus and what their costumes should look like. And by the time they finally arrived home they were all so excited and happy again that they had a hard time convincing their mothers that the eldest boy's arm really was broken. Only in the night, when he began crying, was he was finally taken to the hospital, where the doctor shook his head and informed the family that the boy's forearm was fractured in three places. The arm was set in a cast, and he was sent home. Neighbors came from around the quarter to get a look at it and then smack him on the back of his head for being so foolish.

"Don't be silly," they said. "You can't be an acrobat!"

A year or so later when the boys tried to sneak onto a tram, the second eldest injured himself in an even more dramatic fashion. The boys were trying to jump onto the tram before the doors closed. The eldest and youngest made it, but the middle cousin, instead of making a clean jump through the closing doors, tripped on the running board and fell into the tram as the door closed on his leg. It caused quite a stir, this injury—a major commotion, actually.

A woman screamed, "Stop the tram! Stop the tram!"

Passengers rushed to his side and pulled the doors apart, but somehow in the process a piece of exposed metal cut his leg. He howled and the passengers shouted until the tram operator stopped and radioed for an ambulance. Traffic on the line halted in both directions until the ambulance arrived.

"You've really done it now," the cousins marveled. "They stopped both trams because of you!"

The second eldest was driven away with lights flashing and siren blaring. He smiled and waved at his cousins as he was placed on board. Seventeen stitches later, when the family collected him and returned home, neighbors from around the quarter came by to whistle at the puffy scar on his leg and then smack him on the back of the head for being so foolish.

"What kind of children are you? You stopped the trams in both directions for more than an hour. I had to walk!"

So the boys were used to injuries, and if anything, it was expected of them. The youngest one's head injury was only the latest, but it would still take time to tell whether it stood up in the annals of their remembered accidents. It was certainly promising.

After running away from their altercation with Elza, it took thirty minutes of stumbling and crouching close to walls and shadowy corners before the boys made it back to the Roma quarter. Thirty minutes was twice as long as usual, but the gash on little Pisti's head caused them to move gingerly. The wound was deep on his forehead above his right eyebrow. The skin was torn, and he was bleeding profusely.

"Oooh, Pisti, you look just like a boxer!" said the middle cousin.

"A bad boxer," the eldest said, "who lost the fight."

"She was bigger than him," the middle child protested.

"He leaned back instead of ducking!" the eldest countered. "Everybody knows you're supposed to duck. Uncle told us so!"

Pisti shrugged at them. He remembered the boxing lesson, but he couldn't see how it would have mattered.

The boys stopped and the eldest held Pisti's face in his hands. There would be a purple knot in a few days and maybe even a scar left behind after it healed, but there probably wouldn't be a trip to the hospital. Pisti's eyes darted left and right. Still, they weren't quite sure what to make of this. Nobody outside their neighborhood had ever laid a hand on them before, nobody outside the number of Roma who lived near them, and certainly not a woman. Such violence on the outside was an almost unimaginable thing. Of course, it had been *threatened*. Brooms had been brandished, and curses hurled, but never had an aggressive hand been laid on them.

That's not the way it was done. When Jesus stumbled to Golgotha with his cross over his shoulder, a Gypsy picked his pocket. The Son of God did not smite him. He turned his head and looked away. He looked away! He let them take whatever it was the Romans had left him with.

In their lives the boys had only ever heard of violence happening once, when a gang of shaven-headed thugs had attacked a Roma girl outside a beer garden in the city park. This particular gang of hooligans had been harassing Gypsies for a few months anyway. Nobody knew where they had come from, but they had settled in Delibab like the crows that invaded the skies every winter. They were angry young men who shouted and postured and threatened anyone who was different—unemployed right-wing nationalists who hated leftist governments, free-trade markets, and their increasingly global economy. In fact, this had been the topic of conversation when the fifteen-year-old girl walked past. The men had suddenly stopped speaking and had followed her with their eyes. A pair of hooded fledglings, still trying to make a name for themselves within the group, had left the beer hall and followed her a few meters into the park. They had made cat calls until she had quickened her pace. Once they were all out of sight, the young men had attacked her, punched her a handful of times, and left her in a battered pile behind an oak tree. Then they had run back to the beer hall and shown the others the bruises on their knuckles. The gang had celebrated their victory and congratulated one another with another round of beers.

When the girl had reached home and told her father, a Roma boss, what had happened, the hooligans' fate had been sealed. Within minutes, calls were made and a second gang of men arrived at the beer hall carrying clubs, pipes, and even samurai swords. The sight of angry Gypsies with eyes blazing, gold teeth flashing, and

Samurai swords gleaming was paralyzing. The blades sang shrilly as they slashed through the air. The skinheads were shocked at the sudden appearance, and what ensued wasn't a brawl so much as the act of a redemptive and treacherous Roma god. It was a blur of action made human only by angry roaring and cries of pain. Witnesses who were there, who managed to avoid the Gypsy wrath—because as far as the Roma were concerned, everyone sitting in that beer hall was fair game—said it was over in sixty seconds. Sixty seconds! But when it *was* over, teeth had been stomped out and kept as booty, eyes had been gouged, a finger had been cleaved, and men had been scarred. And also, in one final act of retribution for the beer-hall owner who had allowed the thugs drinking space, who had always been nasty with the women and children who came by to beg out front, all of his kegs of beer were carried off—including four kegs of expensive Czech pilsner. The Gypsies vanished before the police arrived; the skinheads left the city after that and moved to a nearby village.

So this was the incident the boys had for comparison. But, in their case, they weren't anyone's precious daughter and they weren't related to the boss. They were three dirty cousins who worked the Centrum and the train station for spare change and cigarette butts, and Elza wasn't like those thugs. Roma *might* be upset; they might not. Either way, nobody was going to knock on Elza's door holding a pipe, much less a samurai sword.

Her explosion had surprised and offended them. She was usually one of the nicer people along their route, and so they couldn't really understand what to make of it all, or what the fallout might be.

It was dark out as they headed home, but the Centrum was bright with street lamps and traffic. Evening noise from bars and restaurants wafted over them. They stopped every so often to wipe blood out of their injured cousin's eyes using their fingers or sleeves.

They brushed past pedestrians, and while people cast glances at the boys, nobody stopped them or said anything to them.

"Pisti? Pisti? Are you still breathing? Don't stop breathing. Do you think you're dying?"

"I don't think so."

"How can you be sure? Boxers die all the time and don't even know it."

Pisti stopped walking and pinched himself. He seemed satisfied with what he felt and he shrugged at his cousins.

"Did the restaurant lady ever try to kill us before?" he asked

"I don't think so," the eldest cousin said. "I don't remember that she did."

"She was angry with that fat man," said the other.

"Was she?" Pisti asked and wiped his brow.

"Sure she was. This is all his fault, and now we're going to catch hell when we get home."

The cousins considered their dilemma. The two older boys stopped walking and set Pisti down carefully against a wall. They scanned the sidewalk for cigarette butts.

"We're going to be in trouble, anyway, if we don't get home soon." Pisti said from the ground. "We're late."

Not finding any butts worth salvaging, the boys agreed with Pisti and hoisted him up again. They made a last push to their house, and when they arrived, they opened the slatted gate and stepped into the courtyard. They could hear their mothers' voices in the kitchen. The women were arguing. They hesitated a little as they ascended the stairs. They smelled cooking. Their mothers were preparing a goulash and had thrown some old beef medallions into a pan along with onions, sliced carrots, potatoes, and caraway seeds. The boys sniffed the food, and their stomachs growled, but they were frozen in place. They were too afraid to go inside, but couldn't bear to leave. Their mothers, quite frankly, were formidable—stout and mean. They were women with loud mouths, meaty palms, and sausage-like fingers that the boys knew the power of all too well.

The cousins looked at Pisti, who was holding his forehead. At least he'd make it through this injury without everyone smacking him on the head. They stood a moment longer at the threshold hoping to hear a third voice, the soft voice of their youngest aunt, Angela, the flower girl. They might be able to get her attention and hide behind her skirt. She was often the kindest of the adults. She had once bought them all chocolate eggs with prizes inside. They listened for her, but didn't hear her. She was still out.

"We might as well get it over with," Pisti said.

"You don't think you're dying?"

"I don't think so."

"Could you make believe that you are?"

"I could," Pisti said. "You think I should?"

"Yeah. Play it up. Maybe that'll keep them off our backs. Just for a little while."

Pisti shook his head. "They'll make me go to bed! I'm hungry."

His cousins put their hands on his shoulders.

"We'll save you some food. Promise. And the next time we find smokes, you can get the first drag. You don't have to smoke the filter."

Pisti considered this. It was a good deal.

"Promise?"

The cousins nodded, and so Pisti smiled and let out a low moan. He followed that up with real tears. His cousins smiled. Pisti was the most brilliant performer, his cousins thought admiringly. He would have been great in the circus. He held his hand to his head and wobbled. The boys grabbed onto him. They had the good, dramatic idea of wiping his blood on their own cheeks.

"Mama," the eldest called out. "Mama, come out. Come quickly. Pisti is hurt!"

They could hear the women in the kitchen stop talking, and they heard a dish clatter. Two women appeared in the doorway and jockeyed to get through. These were wholly bloated women, sisters endowed with swells around their hips and bellies and peaks for bosoms who somehow weren't soft to touch. They were as solid as mountainsides. Renata and Mona, infamous in the quarter for the advice they sold. They made their living reading cards, offering protection from the evil eye, or telling fortunes. And while their customers didn't think they were particularly good at it, they were better than nothing, so . . .

Renata made it through the threshold first, and when she saw her nephew holding his head and wobbling on his feet, when she saw her own son covered in his—and by extension, her—blood, she momentarily lost all the color in her face. She shouted and reached for the little boy.

"What happened?" she shrieked at them and pawed at Pisti. She enveloped him in her thick arms.

Her sister Mona made it through the threshold and was also taken aback at the sight of the three boys covered in blood, and not knowing what to do, she started smacking the other two boys on their heads. The boys tried to cover themselves, but Mona's balled fists came falling down on them like a rockslide.

"This is how you bring your littlest cousin home? This is how you look out for him? This is how you bring a poor orphan back to us?"

The boys tried running but they were surrounded by so much flesh that they couldn't help but bounce back into the melee of hands. Their heads were thumped and thwacked like drums.

"It wasn't us," they shouted. "We didn't do it."

Renata lifted her nephew and carried him inside the house.

"Be careful," Mona warned. "He could have a brain injury. It happens that way with boxers all the time."

Renata carried Pisti to a bed in the back room and put a cover over him.

"Don't move," she said. "I'm going to clean you up."

She went back to the kitchen to get a wet cloth. She could hear the others outside. The boys were still being walloped. Mona was beating the information out of them.

"What happened?"

"The restaurant lady tried to kill him!"

Renata scowled as she ran the cloth under the tap. She shook her head angrily. Who hits a child? And an orphan at that!

"It wasn't our fault," the boys continued. "It was the restaurant lady. The one who lets Angela sell flowers. We asked her for money and she swung at us like a crazy person."

Renata considered this. Angela often said that the restaurant lady was a nice woman. In fact, Angela was the one who had suggested the boys beg there. Could it really have been a violent attack? There had to be some mistake. She would ask the uncles to look into it.

"We'll let the uncles deal with her," she announced. "When they come by later, we'll tell them all about it. They'll make her pay. There might be an opportunity here."

Mona liked the idea. She smiled at her sister.

The boys looked at each other and grimaced. Their game had not gone as planned; somebody might knock on Elza's door after all. Mona had stopped beating them when the uncles were mentioned. If they changed their story now, she might resume; when she got tired, Renata would start. Then when the uncles came, they might just finish them off. The boys looked at each other and silently decided to keep their mouths shut. Mona straightened her housedress and told them to go inside. They scrambled straight to the stove, to the pan, to try and sneak a medallion of glistening beef, but Renata shouted at them and sent them to the back room.

"No dinner tonight," she said. "We're going to serve that to your uncles."

The boys pouted as they made their way to the room. Pisti sat up when they came in.

"Did it work? Did you bring me anything?"

His cousins slammed the door and threw themselves on the ground. They cursed and stomped the floor with their feet.

"No dinner," they said. "And now the uncles are going to make the restaurant lady pay."

Pisti stiffened. He looked at his cousins.

"Why?"

"My mother's idea. She said there might be an opportunity. I just want some meat."

"Poor restaurant lady," Pisti said.

"Oh well. Serves her right," the eldest cousin sniffed.

The uncles were the only people in the world the boys were truly afraid of. They also weren't really uncles. They were called uncles because—this was an untraditional family arrangement—it was unclear in the tangle of limbs and exchanged fluids between two brothers and two sisters who had sired whom, and which child could call which man Daddy without offending one or the other. As for Pisti's parents, they had actually been married, but they had died in a runaway taxi when he was a baby.

In the old days, a decade or so earlier, the uncles had been day laborers who woke early in the morning to catch the workers' train three hours to a cannery outside Budapest. Since then, however, since the changes had washed over the country, they had been left to scrounge about for odd jobs or the occasional hustle. Now they worked in a new employment program part-time as general laborers. They went wherever the city needed hands to do physical work. They could just as easily remove broken branches and obstructions from the tram line as clean cages at the city zoo. In fact, they'd been doing the latter for the past six weeks, and when the men stopped by in the evening they often smelled like the lion or the bear; but they also came with popcorn and sunflower seeds they had swiped, and so the boys were usually happy to see them.

The first uncle was short and round, as corpulent as either of the sisters, as corpulent as the planet Jupiter. He liked to tell people that it was a thyroid condition—something he had overheard a woman explaining to her husband on a train ride. This uncle lumbered and supported himself with a metal cane. He was the reason they were so often stuck cleaning out animal cages. He was of little use to the work crews otherwise. He couldn't move quickly enough.

His brother, the second uncle, was thin and tall, freakishly so. He was ghoulish looking and pale—a real, bloodsucking Transylvanian, the sisters liked to wink and tease. He wore a knockoff track suit and the same green hunter's cap everywhere he went. He wore sandals during every season. And he rarely spoke. He just stood behind his corpulent brother, wore a taciturn expression, and stared blankly into space. His purpose was to menace—still and tall and taciturn, like a statue wearing a death mask—until he was required to lunge in and emphasize his corpulent brother's point.

The two men visited weekly. They came by to check on the women, to check on their children, maybe grab something to eat or sell, or maybe convince one of the women she needed a poke. They lived outside of the city in an even more run-down quarter.

When they came by that night, Renata and Mona called Pisti and the boys out of bed. The three of them walked into the kitchen and were instructed to tell the story of how Pisti had hurt himself.

"Lookit, I don't want you to spare any detail," their corpulent uncle said. His finger was wagging at them. "I want you boys to tell your loving uncles exactly how this happened."

The ghoulish uncle stood behind him and stared down at the little ones. They looked at him and immediately began crying.

"None of that, now," the corpulent uncle said. "None of that. Lookit, Uncle's just concerned for you, is all. Tell him what happened."

"Nothing happened," Pisti muttered.

"What's that? Come again? You shouldn't lie."

The two other boys decided they had no choice but to talk.

"We went to the restaurant," the eldest boy said. "The one where Angela sells the flowers you get her from the graveyard. We went there and asked for money or something to eat. The restaurant lady is nice sometimes. But tonight she came out and was scary. When she saw us she just swung. I ducked, but Pisti leaned back. She caught him and he fell and hit his head."

"Criminal!" Renata screeched.

"What a horrible woman!" Mona shouted. They had decided now that it was best to urge the uncles to action.

"You sure?" the corpulent uncle asked. "You sure that's all that happened?"

"I'm sure, Uncle," the eldest cousin said. "She saw us and swung. She started swinging."

"Why did you lean back?" the corpulent uncle asked Pisti. "Didn't we teach you how to fight? Someone swings, you duck. Always duck. Never lean back."

The goulish uncle nodded.

"What do you think?" Renata asked. "Will you go and talk to her? Maybe he needs to see a doctor. Doctors are expensive." She winked at her sister.

The uncles looked at Pisti. The gash had clotted by now, and his forehead had turned green.

"Do we have a camera?"

The uncles tore through the house looking for a camera. They found one and ran out to buy film at the corner store.

"How about another little loan?" the corpulent one asked The Shopkeeper. "You'll get it back and then some."

The Shopkeeper sighed and rolled his eyes.

"It took you six months to get the money back to me last time!" he said.

The brothers smiled. The corpulent one took his watch off and placed it on the counter.

"Lookit, a very special watch," he said. "Hold it as collateral."

The Shopkeeper picked up the watch and scoffed. He tossed it back.

"I don't want your poxie watch. Cash only. And I don't want to come looking for it." He took some money from the till and counted it out for them. He wrote it in a ledger. The brothers left with the cash and the roll of film. When they returned to the cottage, they put Pisti back into bed, covered him, and made him lie very still with his eyes closed. They took pictures of him that way. They patted the other boys on their heads and ordered them all to pack some belongings. Then they went back to the kitchen.

"We'll get these developed and then we'll go talk to her in a week or so. Why don't you all come to our place tonight? Just in case she stops by," the corpulent brother said. "Lookit, let her get worked up a little. It'll make it easier to lay into her. I don't believe a thing the boys say, but the kid looks terrible. I think there's an opportunity to make real money here. What do you think, Stretch?"

His brother nodded. Mona served them their goulash. The boys could hear them slurping down their dinner from the back room.

"Bastards," the boys muttered.

Eleven

Elza could not sleep that night. Instead, after she finally got everyone out of the restaurant and went home, she spent the rest of her evening pacing nervously around her flat. She was slick with sweat and covered in food stains, but she didn't change into her casual clothing. She was stuck as she was—distraught and panicked. She poured herself a straight vodka. *What a mess*, she thought. It was all worse than when she'd started. She now had problems she could never have imagined only a few days earlier.

At one point during the night, she looked out her bedroom window expecting to see a police car pull up in front of her building. It was only a matter of time. Though the Motorcycle Officer had dismissed the whole affair with the bloodied boy, she now felt sure other authorities would come for her. She looked at a wall clock. The boy would go to the hospital, surely. He would explain the cause of the injury, or bystanders would tell someone. Elza stuck her torso out the window now and looked left and right along the promenade. Where were the police? She looked at the hotel across the street, thought about the Critic sleeping there, and felt her stomach sink in disgust. The Critic and the professors would check out of the hotel in the morning and there was no way she could make herself face them. She couldn't bring herself to see them off, even after all her professors had done for her.

She poured a second drink, or maybe it was a third. She thought of the Sous-Chef. At least *that* was one situation that had been resolved. Of course, she would have to find a replacement. But as she sipped from her glass and stared out the window, she felt honestly relieved on that point.

Nothing was happening outside. Everything was still. Nobody was looking for her. Nobody wanted her. Was it really so unimportant? Was hurting that child really so inconsequential, like everything else in her life? Elza couldn't imagine that was the case, so she stayed at her window the rest of the night expecting, and hoping, the worst would come pulling up out of the shadows. Maybe she should turn herself in to the police. Offer to pay the doctor's bills. She remembered their home. *How would a poor family manage that? Without a little extra, the doctor might not do as good a job. He might shunt them off onto someone else less experienced. Something. I should do something!*

But Elza didn't move. She sat and rubbed her eyes and waited. She peeled off her socks. She knew Pisti by name now, but she realized she didn't know the other boys' names. Didn't even know the flower girl's name. She had seen these people consistently for at least five years now. Why didn't she know their names?

When the sun rose, Elza was still sitting at her window, and she was so wound up and pensive that when the first tram's bell jangled, she jumped. She watched it pass below like a lumbering metal centipede. It rattled out of the Centrum and on to the rest of the city to pick up the bleary-eyed masses. Elza looked up at the clock on the church tower and calculated the time it would take for her to make a quick call on the boy. She stormed out of her apartment and hurried to the Roma quarter.

The rosy morning light reflected on the glass of the storefronts, and as she hurried along the desolate sidewalks she could smell the bakeries opening. The rich aroma of yeast and sugar wafted out to the sidewalks in front of the shops. It was a comforting smell, and she allowed herself to think that all was not lost. A person might always start again, she reminded herself. Hadn't her own life shown her that? Hadn't the lives of people around her shown her that? Hadn't history shown her that? There was nothing keeping a person from starting over again, if she had to. As long as she was breathing, why not? Elza thought about this as she hurried toward the Roma quarter. *If I could just do one good thing.* She thought of the little boy. *Elza, choose one good thing and do it!*

When she arrived in the Roma quarter at the cottage where she had seen the flower girl enter and the boys playing, she was resolved to make amends and offer assistance. She peered between the slats of wood. There was no movement in the courtyard, nor was there any sound of life coming from inside. She walked along the fence peering between the slats, trying to get a better vantage point, hoping to hear the sound of children's voices. Oh, how she hoped for any sound, but there was nothing. Finally, she rapped against the gate with the flat of her hand. She called out. She rapped against the gate again until the whole fence shook. She hoped the whole thing would tip over, would fall, so that then she could rush to the door and bang against that. But the house remained still. There was no answer. It didn't seem like anybody was there.

A corner store up the street was open and Elza walked inside. Two men were talking in low voices. They were writing figures into a ledger in front of them. They nodded at the ledger, cursed it, and gestured at it as though it were insulting them. Elza could tell the men were arguing about something. However, they were speaking so rapidly and with such a strong accent, peppered with Roma words, that she had trouble following them. They stopped what they were doing when they noticed her standing there, and they looked at her as though she had materialized out of nowhere.

"Can I help you?" the Shopkeeper asked suspiciously and looked behind her to see if she was alone. Elza could feel the other man looking her over as well.

Elza straightened her hair and flashed a smile. She gestured in the direction of the cottage and the gate.

"I'm looking for the people who live in that cottage there. Do you know how I can reach them?" she asked.

The Shopkeeper walked to the door and looked out at the house. He shook his head.

"Them? I have no idea," he said. "They're all pains in the rear, though. I saw the boys stumbling home last night. They seemed drunk. Just little kids, mind you. So sad. And then the whole lot of them left in a flurry late last night. I have no idea where. You need to find them?"

Elza felt light-headed. She thought about the boys having to stumble home. It was too horrible. "I do need to find them," she said.

The Shopkeeper looked her over again. His face was sharp and chiseled, and his hair was short, but his paunch stuck out ahead of him and he had a thick moustache. He seemed well off. He wore an expensive track suit and new trainers. He appraised her a moment and said, "Yeah, well, they owe me money, so I need to find them too."

The second man standing in the shop consulted the ledger and nodded. He looked at Elza. "If they owe you money, you're going to have to wait your turn," he said.

Elza looked down at her shoes; she had an idea.

"I owe *them* money!" she announced.

The two men straightened up when she said this. They looked at Elza even more suspiciously.

"You owe them?" the Shopkeeper asked. "You sure about that?"

"That's the house of a young woman who sells flowers and three little boys, yes?"

The Shopkeeper nodded.

"They did some work for me. I owe them ten thousand forints."

The two men exchanged another glance.

"They worked?" the Shopkeeper asked with raised eyebrows. He pulled the ledger from his assistant and consulted it. He remembered the previous night when the fathers had come in looking for a roll of film. They had been acting cagier than normal, the tall one looking around and the short one sweating and trying to contain his giddiness. He had given them what they needed along with an additional forty-five hundred forints in cash. At least, that's what the ledger told him. Six thousand forints would settle the debt. He looked more closely at Elza. The woman was up to something, and she looked scared. Police scared. Harried, filthy, and scared. She smelled like she'd been drinking. He also thought she looked like she wanted to be absolutely anywhere but standing there in this shop or in this neighborhood. He was certain he could squeeze the money out of her.

"Look," he said. "That bunch of misfits is always in here asking for money. The men clean up at the zoo sometimes, and the women, except for that flower girl, go around this whole neighborhood giving bad advice and charging people for it. It'll be a couple of months before I see any of my money. Why don't you be a good friend and pay their debt for them? Eight thousand forints. I'll wipe it from my books here and trust me, you'd be doing them a favor. No need to stick around. I'll wipe it off the books and let them know you paid it for them."

Elza looked at the Shopkeeper and the second man. He was nodding at her as though it were a good deal.

"What do they owe you money for?" Elza asked. She looked around. There were a few items on the shelves beside her. Nothing that could sustain a large family, though.

"Groceries," the Shopkeeper said. "Groceries and cash when they came up short on their rent. It's a habit with them. Look, lady, you don't want to get mixed up with that bunch. They're the kind who give Gypsies a bad name. You look like a nice lady. You don't want to be mixed up with them. Pay their debt and you'd be doing all of us a favor."

Elza hesitated. She turned her head just in time to spot the flower girl walking from the cottage.

"Oh!" Elza exclaimed to the Shopkeeper. "There she is now! Let me check with her."

She turned to head out, but the Shopkeeper brushed past her and sprinted out the door like an Olympian. He was shouting, calling out to Angela as she crossed the street. Angela heard him and quickened her pace trying to get away, but the Shopkeeper caught up with her and herded her against a parked car. She was pinned between him and the vehicle. He talked forcefully to her and it seemed for a moment as if he might even strike her. Elza hurried quickly after him, calling out. Angela looked the Shopkeeper defiantly in the eyes.

"She says she's going to pay your debt!" the Shopkeeper bellowed. "I say let her pay it. What do you say? I say let her leave the money with me."

The Shopkeeper looked at Elza, beside him now. "You'll pay the full eight thousand forints?"

"I'll give you ten thousand," she said, "for the children's groceries next week."

The Shopkeeper looked at Angela. Angela raised an eyebrow.

"Maybe I should take the money home," Angela said. "We can come by and pay you what we owe later."

"That's fine also," Elza said. "I'd prefer it that way, really. I'd prefer to give it to you."

"Bah," the Shopkeeper said and placed himself squarely between them. "You're both crazy. She can just give *me* the money. You guys have run too long without paying."

Elza was trying to catch Angela's attention and her head popped up in various places from behind the Shopkeeper. "How's little Pisti?" she asked. "Is he your brother? Is he all right? What's your name? I'm sorry I never asked. It was a terrible accident."

"Look," the Shopkeeper also spoke to Angela. "I don't know who this lady is, but you tell your sisters and their blokes that I want my money. One way or another you lot are going to pay off your debt. You should let her pay it for you right now."

"You'll get your money," Angela sneered and tried to push him away. "Just as soon as I get it from her and talk to my sisters. They're not home right now."

Elza maneuvered herself between them.

"You have to believe me that it was an accident," she said to the flower girl.

Angela looked incredulously at both of them. Neither one was making any sense. She had been out all night at a party, had only just arrived from her boyfriend's village in the countryside and stopped in to pick up some clean clothes. She shook her head and looked toward her cottage.

"Nobody is there," he said, "because they all cut out last night. So, you're going to let her pay me. Do you hear me? Right now."

"I don't know what came over me!" Elza was still babbling. "Is Pisti all right? Maybe I should speak to your mother."

The Shopkeeper had heard enough. He turned to Elza and poked her with a finger.

"Look here, nutjob," he said. "I don't know what you're doing around here, but we're busy. Whatever problem you've got, you can take care of it on your own time. Right now the problem is my eight thousand forints. If you're so desperate to help them, you should start there."

He was jamming his finger into Elza's brachial plexus and breathing angrily in her face. Elza felt dizzy. Without thinking she pushed him away as hard as she could. She pushed him so hard, in fact, that one hand pressed deep into his belly fat and the other pressed into his nose. He winced and took a step back.

"Get away from us," she shouted and pushed him a second time on the chest, causing him to take another step back. She was about to hammer his nose with her fist, but before she could, the Shopkeeper grimaced and threw a quick jab straight at her mouth. It was the punch that he leveled on deadbeats; it was the punch he had been working himself up to lay on Angela.

Elza went sprawling backward into the parked car. She was shocked silent. The Shopkeeper was visibly angry now. Trembling. As for Angela, she didn't stick around to see what happened. She took this moment of confusion to bolt off. Elza just had time to reach out for her; but she felt only a wisp of hair slip through her fingertips.

"Please don't leave me here," she said weakly.

Angela ran away, as quickly as she could. She went back to the train station and jumped without a ticket onto the first train leaving.

"I warned you to stay out of it," the Shopkeeper loomed over Elza. He was looking around uncomfortably. He was worried now that she might go to the police. His friend came out of the shop and pulled him back by his shoulder. "If you come around here looking for trouble, you're going to find it!"

Elza was weeping silently and wobbled to a full stance. She reached into her pocket. She pulled out a handful of notes. The Shopkeeper waved his hands and shook his head.

"Oh, no! I don't want that now," he said. "You'll come back with the cops and say I robbed you. Just get out of here, would you? Don't come back around here."

"Take it!" Elza screamed. "You stupid peasant, take it! Let them buy some groceries next week."

The Shopkeeper wouldn't take the money. Elza held the bills up for him to get a good look at, and then she crumpled them and threw them at his face. The money fell to the ground. A crumpled, salmon-colored five-thousand-forint note rolled in the breeze. The Shopkeeper's silent friend bent over quickly to pick up the bills before they rolled away. Elza looked in the direction in which Angela had run.

"They're trouble, lady. They'll only make trouble for you," the Shopkeeper murmured. "Whatever you *think* you owe them, you don't. Just get out of here."

Elsa was woozy and shaken, and the Shopkeeper reached an arm out to steady her. When his fingers touched her, Elza turned and walked off without a word. She held her jaw in her hand and nursed it. She returned to her flat, taking pains to avoid passing the hotel. She went up to her apartment and fell onto her bed. At ten A.M. her phone rang, but she refused to answer it. She knew it was the professors calling to meet her before they left for the lake. She couldn't do it. She dropped her head back down and wept until she fell asleep. More than anything she wept because it was confirmed now: she couldn't do a single thing right. She couldn't do one good thing.

Twelve

In the two weeks following the incident at Tulip, Elza's life unraveled in such a way that it seemed to be a scheme devised by overzealous kitchen Furies. They were incredibly thorough, the ravenous old bats. Muscle by muscle they knew exactly how to dissect the fibers and sinew until she was a flaccid, flabby wreck. They knew exactly where to incise her—where to eviscerate her—and their cracked and yellowed nails poked her apart and gutted her as easily as though she were a halibut prepared for cooking, about to be lightly seasoned and steamed over a bed of onions for serving. Never in her life had Elza experienced or seen things unravel for a person so quickly.

Angela, the flower girl, hadn't returned to the restaurant after that day with the Shopkeeper. Of course, since Elza had lost two of her chefs and hadn't started looking for replacements, she had to close Tulip in the evenings, so that might have been the reason. But for a week, Elza had visited the Roma quarter every day, and she hadn't seen Angela there either. Nor had she seen the boys. Their cottage remained desolate, and she'd come to know the slatted fence well—had grown intimate with the feel of the wood against her palm from the constant slapping and calling out, had become familiar with the littered courtyard and its strewn newspapers and overflowing trash bin.

She haunted the neighborhood so often—in the early morning and then again in the afternoon, when the sun was rising and setting, when the light was pink then golden—that residents there quickly began to recognize and expect her.

And somehow a unique version of what had transpired between Elza and little Pisti began to spread around the neighborhood. Now, the adults, try as they might, couldn't convince their children to leave their homes when Elza was about.

"I'm not going anywhere while that smelly witch is outside," the children argued. "She might try to eat me as well!"

For these children all believed the gossip they had heard, the stories *they* had invented and told one another, about how it had come to pass that a kid as streetwise as little Pisti should disappear. And the details of this story changed with the light of each day, changed when the light was pink or golden. The details twisted into grotesque contortions, folded over, doubled back, and leapt to dizzying heights of fantasy. But there was one punctiform nail on which the entire imagined narrative hung, and everyone under the age of twelve knew it—knew it the way they knew that despite tricks of light, the sun itself is always yellow! And this singular detail that was repeated, that echoed in a day or so throughout the quarter, this belief they all shared was that somehow, on the night he disappeared, as in ancient legends from Transylvanian woods, Elza had lured Pisti into her restaurant and eaten him. Not metaphorically, either! Not symbolically or metaphysically. Elza had eaten him, plain and simple. She had boiled his bones and sucked out the marrow; she had used his blood and liver for pudding; and she had spiced the scant meat on his ribs for stuffed cabbages she later served to her customers. First, the children said, she had lured him in with the promise of pocket money. Then, once he was there, she had offered him a bowl of poisoned cherries. It was this simple. He had sat and eaten the cherries while he jangled the money in his pocket. When he became groggy, Elza had smiled sweetly at him and sung him a lullaby. Pisti had stretched. He had yawned. She had tousled his hair gently. She had petted him. And when he finally had dozed off, she had pulled a carving knife from beneath her chef's coat and butchered him with one deft stroke.

"Ooh, the stinky witch!" the children crowed to one another. "She keeps his head in her refrigerator. He is there right now. They talk to one another! And then she tried to catch the other boys and eat them and put their heads in the refrigerator, too, so Pisti wouldn't be lonely, and that's why the family left. So I'm not going out there! I'm not going to look for money today. I'm very afraid. I'm not going anywhere!"

This refusal of young labor to leave the home had the same effect on the neighborhood as any labor strike would have on a multinational factory floor. Everything stopped. Nobody was available to carry things. Nobody brought loose change in from the streets. Nobody delivered messages. The entire economic fabric of the neighborhood came undone. Everything was silent in the quarter except for Elza slapping on the gate and calling out for a family that had disappeared.

"Hello! Oh, please. Hello?"

The adults sighed and watched Elza pacing to and fro and cursed her under their breaths.

And when it became clear that curses wouldn't deter the woman from walking and wailing through their neighborhood, wouldn't stop her from asking people about the whereabouts of the family, the next phase of judgment was unabashed ridicule.

"The devil can stand everything but ridicule," mothers reasoned. "Let us laugh at her."

So women began hurling insults when Elza walked past. They spat. They threw garlic, and if they didn't have garlic, then onions, and if they ran out of onions, they threw scallions or radishes.

"May you stay forever barren!" was one of their favorite insults. It came right before they tossed a handful of roots at her. Elza, who wondered how they knew she didn't have children to begin with, thought this curse a particularly strange one.

"Yes, yes," she answered. "That's very clever, but I never wanted to be a mother anyway."

"Because you're barren and dusty!" came the response. "May your baby suffocate in your womb for what you've done!"

"May men wither in your dry socket and never find release!" shouted others, "May they go blind from looking at you."

"Barren!"

"Dry!"

Roma men heard the cursing and came out laughing. They found these insults to be particularly humorous, and they peeked out from wherever they were to take a longer look at Elza—the barren and dusty, child-eating chef.

Expecting to see some type of ogre, some monstrous, pendulous woman with seven guts, a sloping face, and a wide mouth, they were surprised to see this attractive petite brunette standing at the gate instead. "She's not a bad sort at all. She's all right."

"Listen," they called out to her when their women had stopped. "You don't mind them. I've never withered once! It isn't even possible. Give me three days and I'll sort you out. Three days and I'll give you a baby. Three days and you'll never want to eat another child again!"

After a few days of this Elza stopped responding to the specific insults. She became desparate.

"Have you seen the little boy who lives in that cottage? Have you seen his family? Please, can you help me? I'm looking for them. I'm looking for him."

"You ate him!" the children cried from behind their bedroom windows.

"Barren and dusty," the women ridiculed.

"Three days," the men teased. "Pregnant in three—two days!"

And then doors and windows slammed shut, or people turned their backs on her and ignored the rest of her queries.

So after seven days of this, Elza gave up. She stopped visiting the neighborhood. She resigned herself to the thought that maybe she would never find out what had happened to Pisti. *Maybe I should feel relieved*, she supposed, but couldn't convince herself as she walked away for the last time, her feet dragging and her shoulders drooping. Still, if a family didn't want to be found, what could she do? She had plenty enough to contend with at her restaurant.

Thirteen

Dora and the Sous-Chef were making great strides in preparing the grand opening of their new restaurant, the Three Roses. And they both agreed that the annual flower carnival—the summer's high point in Delibab—would be the perfect day to open for business. The carnival was famous throughout the region and attracted teeming crowds from across the countryside who brought their families to wander around the promenade, to shop, or to watch the parade as it snaked its way through the city. It was a day-long affair, full of carnival rides and parade floats made of flowers of all kinds, and it took city planners a full year to prepare for.

And in opening their brasserie on the promenade, right along the parade route, with seating out front on the sidewalk, the Sous-Chef was nearly giddy with excitement. He smiled broadly when he thought of the money they stood to make.

The young couple worked hard at coming up with their menu, and they were happy with the selections they decided upon, especially with the colorful and exotic meals they invented—selections like their cold lemon-pepper duck breast salad, or their hearty paella and gazpacho combination. Delibab had never seen concoctions like that at any restaurant. It would be a global eatery, gourmet-style food served fast. The entrées were chosen precisely because they were so easy to prepare, yet as the young couple tested them in the kitchen, they made them whimsical and wondrous. They only needed a handful of entrées anyway, they decided, because the true focus of the Three Roses was going to be its desserts—desserts and pastries.

"The smell of melting sugar is going to draw people," the Sous-Chef said to his soon-to-be father-in-law when they went over the menu with him. "We don't need too many entrées. Just something interesting to taste before it's time for dessert. When we have built the brand enough, then we can take the recipes to the factory and start boxing everything."

So, while their list of entrées was slight, their list of baked goodies was nearly endless. There were to be cakes. So many different types of cakes! Ice-cream cakes covered in freshly whipped heavy cream and fruit. Seven-layer cakes with poppy seed filling and drizzled with chocolate. Cakes layered with marzipan. Apple slices. Plum slices. Yeast dough with Bavarian cream. Puff pastries. Strudels. Turnovers. They would have a large display case inside with all the bakery available for dining in or to taking out. They were even going to have marzipan roses. Marzipan roses that looked so real that despite how delicious they were, no one would want to eat them. Wild roses with long stems and ribbons. They hoped to sell bouquets of them at weddings or name-day celebrations. The flowers, Dora's idea, would be made out of balls of almond paste and sugar that she cut into smaller pieces and flattened into little petals. With quick fingers she folded the petals together into a tight bud, gently attaching more and more petals until the rose bloomed in her hand.

"I can make them in any color," she said to the Sous-Chef when she showed it to him. "Isn't it wonderful?"

It was wonderful. The Sous-Chef bit into the rose and it gave way. It practically melted on his tongue. He smiled with pleasure and stroked Dora's shoulders.

"It will be our signature," he said. "Three of these on every table."

Their responsibilities did not end in the kitchen. The young couple was also overseeing the finishing touches of the restaurant's construction. They had settled on a good corner location and had taken the space of three storefronts. They planned the outdoor seating. They chose colors and fixtures. They worked with contractors to ensure that everything was arranged the way they envisioned it.

And as if all of this were not enough to keep the couple busy, the Sous-Chef had come up with an ambitious plan to rent food vending carts the day of the flower carnival and have them set up along the entire parade route. The carts would sell a small selection of waffles and crepes or cakes and cookies. The workers would hand out fliers for the restaurant, good for free coffee.

"We are going to make so much money," the Sous-Chef said. "We can put it toward the new flat."

With only a little less than a month left before the flower carnival, the Sous-Chef was making sure he had the right permits and had enough people to man the carts. He had finally sold his car and his mother's weekend garden as he had planned, and he put all of his own money into this side venture. It kept him up at night, putting all his energy into this idea, but he wanted to prove to Dora (and to her father) that he was industrious, that he was a dedicated partner with good ideas, that he would make a fine husband, a fine addition to the family, and that Dora and he could start off their lives even more comfortably than they would otherwise have been.

He was full-steam on a path of his own making, and he was

happy about it. The only pebble in his shoe was that he found himself thinking about Elza quite often. She squatted in the back of his mind like a forgotten clove of garlic in the icebox that has started to sprout. When he went to City Hall to deliver paperwork, he imagined he saw her sitting in the waiting room looking up at him. When he and Dora were picking out wall colors meeting with the contractors, he imagined he heard Elza's voice in his head telling him which colors to choose. He could not shake these feelings; he could not shake her out of his mind. The bitterness he had felt those few weeks earlier when she had thrown him and Dora out had begun to fade.

Of course, he had no desire to change anything. He was happy with Dora. He was happy where he was. But he wanted to see Elza again. Except, how to arrange something like that now? Dora, for her part, was glad to be done with the entire affair. She talked about her time working at Tulip as though it had been the worst experience of her life. She felt she had been treated shabbily and she often said that she could not understand how he had put up with Elza for so long. The Sous-Chef found Dora's ill will odd, because overall, the years for him had been quite enjoyable. But it would do no good to argue the point, of course.

"I think we should try to hire Elza's dishwasher," he said instead, when he could arrive at no other justification for a visit to Elza, at least no justification he thought would make sense to a young fiancée. He said it as they were walking in their new kitchen and entered the dishwashing section. The kitchen at the Three Roses was enormous and was set up to be as much a bakery as a savory kitchen. Like everything else about the restaurant, it was twice as large as Elza's, and everything in it was made of stainless steel. Nothing makeshift at all. All of it was spotless. All of it had been imported by Dora's father, at great cost, from Germany.

Dora examined the tiled floors for chips and scratches. She made a face at the thought of the Dishwasher.

"He smells," she began. "But he's a very good worker, it's true. If we offered him a little more than Elza pays him, I'm sure we could get him."

The Sous-Chef walked to the new oven and opened it. Six clean racks and heating filaments still shrink-wrapped in plastic. He peeled them off.

"I'll take a walk over there tomorrow evening when they're closing," he offered. "I'll catch up with him when he's leaving. Do you want to come?"

"Ugh—no," Dora said.

"That's fine." The Sous-Chef nodded, relieved. "I'll take care of it."

The next evening he strolled from the Three Roses to Tulip. It was a short walk, only a few minutes. They were practically in the same neighborhood. He knew that once Elza discovered that fact, she would be offended. But the location was just so perfect. Close enough to the hotel. Close enough to the tram stop.

When he arrived, he was surprised to find the restaurant closed. In fact, the posted hours had been changed; the restaurant had been closed since mid-afternoon. He peeked in through the great picture window but didn't see anybody. He left and met Dora at her home.

"That was fast," she said. "What did the Dishwasher say?"

The Sous-Chef was thinking about what the change of hours could mean. He couldn't believe Elza would choose to end her dinner service. What was she thinking? What was she doing?

"It was closed," he said. "Nobody was around. They're only doing lunch."

Dora did not seem as surprised as he was. He followed her to her room, where she changed out of her work clothes and began brushing her hair.

"It's not surprising," she said.

"That doesn't seem odd to you?" he asked.

"Not really," Dora said. "Elza's not really a business person."

The Sous-Chef winced. He couldn't agree with Dora without feeling disloyal to Elza.

"She's a good chef," he said.

Dora stopped brushing and turned to look at him.

"I didn't say she wasn't a good chef," she said. "She's a great chef. One of the best I've met. She's just not a good business person. She's not a good manager. A restaurant owner is a business owner."

The Sous-Chef decided he should listen to what Dora had to say. He had learned quickly that Dora and her family saw things in a way that very few people did, and he was only just getting the hang of it—their sixth sense for noticing inefficiencies.

"Tell me," he said.

"Well, for starters," Dora began. "How about a good manager not sleeping with employees? That seems basic, don't you think? You told me yourself how you had all those good ideas, the same ideas we're using now, and she never listened. She never took you seriously. Didn't you ever wonder why?"

The Sous-Chef nodded. He did remember. He remembered all the times Elza had shut him down, hadn't listened to his suggestions, had dismissed him as if he were a schoolboy . . . or a *plaything*!

"I hadn't thought of that," he said meekly.

"And a good boss and a good manager wouldn't allow creepy line cooks, who are probably criminals to boot, to work in her kitchen."

The Sous-Chef thought of all the arguments with the line cooks. He shook his head. They were terrible, those men. He was glad not to have to deal with them anymore.

"She only lasted ten years because there was no serious competition," Dora said. "But times are different now. Don't get me wrong. She's a fabulous chef. Those recipes are well thought out, and she's a great cook. But she has no idea how to manage a business, and her only luck was that she picked a city in the middle of nowhere when everyone else with talent left! She probably ended dinner because she can't find anyone to replace us. We just spent the last couple of weeks hiring for our kitchen, and it wasn't easy, was it? She won't find anyone because there isn't anybody else in this city who can do our job."

The Sous-Chef knew she was right.

"You're brilliant!" he cried. "You're absolutely perfect."

"Talk to that smelly dishwasher!" Dora resumed brushing her hair. "Honestly, you'll be doing him a favor. If Elza doesn't figure things out, she'll be out of business by autumn."

When the Sous-Chef returned to Tulip the next afternoon he found the Dishwasher locking up. He approached him with newfound purpose and confidence. The two men shook hands and chatted. Upon being asked of the changes, the Dishwasher shook his head and said, "I feel so bad for the old girl. She's lost. We're only open for a long lunch now. I don't know what she's going to do."

The Sous-Chef looked at the locked restaurant and at his reflection in the glass looking back.

"Why hasn't she hired anybody?" he asked. "What is she waiting for?"

"I don't know," the Dishwasher said. "Nobody has really come looking. And it seems her heart's not in it."

The two men looked up at the sign.

"I tried to get her to marry me, you know," the Sous-Chef said. "More than once I asked. I wanted to marry her. I would have many times."

The Dishwasher shook his head. "You were sniffing around the wrong skirt there. She's not the marrying sort. Not at all."

"Why not?"

The Dishwasher tapped his head with a finger.

"She's trapped inside there. That's all. She won't come out. Nobody gets in."

The Sous-Chef considered this. The three years he had spent with her became much clearer to him: the evenings together when she had seemed so uncomfortable with his company, the subtle but sure-handed ways she had kept him at bay. The Sous-Chef realized, for the first time, that he had never truly been her confidant. She hadn't even tried to fake intimacy.

He felt stupid, but he wasn't angry. He thought about his loving fiancée.

"Yes, well, that's all very interesting," he said finally with much clearer-eyed purpose, "but the real reason I came today was because of you. Dora and I would like it very much if you came to work for us. We need someone with experience who can keep everything humming along in the back. We're also certain we can pay you more than what you're making, even with that raise you just got. Are you interested?"

The Dishwasher hemmed and hawed. He talked about loyalty and about his years of service to Elza, but just to be certain they were on the same page, he mentioned to the Sous-Chef what his new salary was; and when the Sous-Chef nodded his understanding, when he didn't blink and offered fifteen percent more, the Dishwasher stopped short and stared at his feet.

"I'd be daft not to take it!" he said to the pavement. "I'd feel terrible, but I'd be daft not to say yes."

"Well, think about it," the Sous-Chef said and reached out for his hand. "But you wouldn't have to wash linens anymore. You wouldn't have to do anything but make sure the kitchen runs smoothly. You'd be our sergeant at arms, and we'd need you to start in a couple of weeks."

The two men shook. The Sous-Chef turned and headed back to his restaurant, his step lighter now that he understood what was what. The Dishwasher, meanwhile, walked away in his own direction, heavier, as though he were carrying a stove over sand.

Fourteen

Elza worked late going over figures in her office and looking for the mathematic miracle that would save her business. However, try as she might—and add as she might—she could not get the numbers to sum up the way she needed them to. There was always a large sunken deficit at the end of her pencil. The extended lunch alone wasn't working. She was sinking.

She sat at her seat and bit her eraser. She changed the order in which she added as though the order made a bit of difference. Maybe she wasn't carrying a one somewhere? She tapped her fingers on the table as though trying to scare a favorable number out of hiding. She looked for it as best she could.

The sound of running water came from the kitchen. It was the Dishwasher. Over the past couple of days he had taken to cleaning *everything* as furiously as he was able. She couldn't understand what he was on about, but he had spent quite a few hours scrubbing tiles, baseboards, and the two prep stations. In truth, the kitchen hadn't looked so good in a long time, and Elza appreciated it. She certainly didn't want to stop him. However, at the same time, it made her uneasy. She tried to ignore the sound and looked at the numbers in front of her. She found she couldn't. She called out to him.

"I think you got everything," she said. "I'm not sure there's anything left to clean."

The water turned off. She heard his footsteps approaching. He was standing at her door looking in, wiping his hands on a towel.

"What's that you say?" he asked.

Elza took the pencil out of her mouth and looked up at him. "I said, I think you got everything. The place is spotless."

The Dishwasher nodded. If he was going to leave her, he was going to leave her in the best way he knew how. He'd accepted the job at the Three Roses. It hadn't taken him long to decide. He called the Sous-Chef the same day they had spoken. Now his only problem was how to break the news to Elza. She had been through so much, and he knew she would not take it well. He had kept putting it off, but now that everything was spotless, as she said, there was nothing left to do.

"What's going on with you?" Elza raised a quizzical eyebrow.

"What? Me? I was just cleaning. Did you see?"

"I saw," Elza said. She got up and walked past him into her kitchen. "It looks splendid."

He followed her as she inspected everything.

"I guess I should have given you a raise sooner," she said.

The Dishwasher absentmindedly wiped down the shiny, clean stovetop. It was now or never, he decided.

"I saw the Sous-Chef the other day," he said. "They're putting the final touches together on their restaurant. They're opening for the flower carnival."

"Ah, I see," Elza said. "That's faster than I expected. Does the competition make you nervous? Is that why you're cleaning?"

"They've sponsored one of the floats for the parade."

"Really!" Elza said. She imagined the Sous-Chef waving from a float, throwing flowers like a triumphant emperor.

"They'll have a lot of work at the restaurant, though." The Dishwasher continued. "It's a large place. They'll have a patio in front."

Elza smiled thinly. "I've seen it going up from my window," she said. She had noticed burly men loitering out in front of it or carrying in fixtures or paint buckets. It looked like a massive project.

The Dishwasher was prattling on about it tirelessly now. She was sorry she'd gotten him on this reverie. He talked about the hand-painted Italian crockery they were importing and the industrial dishwasher they had bought. He told her about the lighting and the tiles and even about the fabric on the chairs. He knew an awful lot about it, she thought . . . an awful lot.

"You seem like you know a lot about it," she said.

"About the new restaurant?" he started. Elza noticed now that he kept looking around him, like a cornered fowl about to have its head lobbed off.

"Yes," she said. "You must have had quite a long conversation to know this much."

The Dishwasher looked wistfully at the doors to the dining room. He nodded. "Well, I visited, actually. They're going to have full eight-hour shifts," he said. "They expect to be very busy. They're going to buy a lot of advertisements in the papers and weeklies."

"Well, I really think that's great for them," she said tersely. She was tired of this. "If you see him again, congratulate him for me. Congratulate them both. We'll have more hours here when we're back on our feet."

There was a beat of silence before the Dishwasher spoke again.

"Yes, about that," he said. "Elza, dear, they've offered me a job."

"What's that?" Elza snapped.

The Dishwasher took in a great big breath and steadied himself before he struck the final blow. "They want me to work with them," he said. "To look after the cleaning and such. They said I'd be their sergeant at arms in the kitchen."

Elza felt dizzy.

"How dare they!" she cried. "They offered *you* a job?"

Now the Dishwasher was taken aback. Why wouldn't they offer him one?

"Yes, dear. A job and a raise!" he said. "They want me to start right away. To start next Monday."

Elza shook her head. She felt betrayed. Had she been so horrible an employer? She'd lost so much already; she couldn't lose the Dishwasher!

"I just gave you a raise," she argued. "When they left, I gave you a raise."

The Dishwasher looked down uncomfortably.

"They've offered more," he said. "Elza, dear, I hate to leave you. But if I take it, I won't have to clean linens for extra money. Do you think you can match them?"

She couldn't. She knew she couldn't. She didn't even have to hear a number. She threw her hands up in defeat.

"Fine," she said. "If it's such a fine opportunity for you then you should take it. Take it! But I really thought you'd be the last person to do this to me. I thought I could count on you."

She turned and marched back to her office.

The Dishwasher looked around.

"I gave it a good cleaning!" he called out. "And, you know, I have a nephew who needs a job. I'm sure he'd do this at my old salary. Maybe even less. It'd be a win-win."

Elza felt her eyes tearing up. She composed herself before turning around and sticking her head out of the office. "Yes," she said.

"That's fine. Send him in. Send him. I guess I have to take anyone I can get now."

The Dishwasher approached her as though he might try and hug her. She stepped back and crossed her arms uncomfortably in front of her. He turned and headed for the exit without another word. She heard the doors close behind him. Then she moaned out loud to herself and kicked her desk.

It was dark out when she finally had the energy to get up from her seat again. She turned out the lights. She locked the door behind her and had started home when she had the uncomfortable feeling of being watched. She turned around. A pair of odd-looking men caught her eye. One was short and round, while the other stood tall and at attention like a maypole. They were standing across the street at the corner of the opposite sidewalk. Though they were quite a distance from her, they were definitely watching her. She stood frozen, unsure of which direction to walk. Something about the way they looked at her made her stomach sink. She wondered what they wanted.

The Round Man pulled at something from behind the Maypole, and Elza went completely white. It was one of the boys! The eldest one. She recognized him straightaway.

Whatever was going on, the boy did not want to be a part of it. Elza watched as the Round Man yanked the boy by his arm. The boy writhed and tried to pull himself free until the Maypole slapped the back of his head. Elza watched the whole thing unfold as though she were in a dream. It was a hot summer night, and the warm air had slowed everything down. The traffic lights and streetlamps caught the haze rising from the street and caused her image of the men to flicker like candle flames.

Elza didn't quite feel afraid. There were pedestrians about and plenty of traffic on the street. But she did feel uncomfortable, and wasn't sure of her next move. It would be best, she felt, if these men did not know where she lived.

Elza saw the boy explaining something to the men. They considered what he said and nodded. Then the Maypole said something and the boy nodded . . . and pointed directly at her. Elza wanted to sink into the ground.

The boy was talking much faster now. Elza watched as his mouth contorted. She wished she could hear what they were saying, what the boy was explaining. She wished she could interject, explain herself, but she didn't want to get any closer. The boy was still pointing at her. Emphatically pointing at her. Thrusting his finger. Jabbing with his index. And every time he did, Elza felt it on her skin and wanted to shrink away. Then he pointed at the curb in front of the restaurant. He pointed at his head. Elza remembered the sound Pisti's head had made when it hit the pavement. She felt suddenly light-headed herself. She was sure now, what he was saying, and sure that the men would set upon her at any moment.

But they didn't seem to be in a hurry. The Round Man stroked his moustache and nodded. He looked up and down the street. The Maypole kept his eyes on Elza.

And Elza, though she had spent a week trying to find them, now that they were in front of her wanted very much for them to disappear again.

But fighting her instinct to escape, Elza approached them. Though her legs were as heavy as frozen sides of beef, she willed them to move. She didn't take her eyes off of the men. She noticed the sandals on the Maypole's feet. She noticed the feather in his green hunter's cap. His track suit had an oil stain on the chest. She noticed the Round Man's metal cane. She noticed that he held it in his right hand and leaned heavily against it. Then Elza looked at the boy. He was not wearing a shirt, only khaki shorts. She tried to catch his eyes, but he shook his head and broke free, an expression of terror on his face, as if she really had eaten his little cousin. The two men tried to grab him, but he was like a panicked rabbit. She heard them call out for him, and then they turned and gave chase. Elza let herself breathe again. The Maypole looked back at her twice, and he squinted his eyes at her threateningly, but she knew they were gone for the evening. Her heart beat in her ears and she looked up at the sky. She forgot about counting figures or the Dishwasher. She forgot about parades and floats. She hurried straight home and locked all the doors behind her. She peeked out her window from behind a curtain.

For several hours she waited to see if they would come back, but they never came. Eventually she went to sleep, though she had unpleasant dreams all night long.

In the morning, first thing, she returned to the Roma quarter and their cottage. It had been more than a week since she had last visited, yet when they saw her approaching, the neighborhood children still scattered for their homes.

"It's the stinky witch!" they shouted. "She's back to eat us."

Elza slapped the gate of the cottage as usual, and as usual there was no answer. She walked to the corner store. The Shopkeeper and his assistant were there. They looked up when she walked in.

"What do you want?" the Shopkeeper asked nervously.

"Is the family back? I saw the eldest boy with two men."

The Shopkeeper sighed. "No. They're not back. They never came back around here. I guess it's a lucky thing for me you left that money behind after all. I would have never seen it again. But I guess now that they're looking for you, you're going to find out what real trouble is. I imagine you'll get to know God fairly soon."

He laughed. He looked to his assistant, who snorted also. Elza left and hurried back to the restaurant. The day would start soon, and she wanted to get through it as quickly as possible. Throughout the lunch service she kept leaving the kitchen to check the dining room and stare out the picture window. Her customers stopped her to offer well wishes and advice, but she couldn't pretend to listen to them, only thanked them absently before returning to the kitchen.

"Not very friendly," one diner barked after her.

"Not friendly at all," said another.

The Motorcycle Officer looked sternly at the disgruntled customers until they quieted and abashedly stared into the day's soup.

Elza stayed late again washing her own dishes. The men hadn't returned. She walked slowly home, always looking behind her.

They didn't come the next day either, or the day afterward, or the day after that. Eventually, she stopped expecting them, and then one morning when she was headed in early to start the prep work, she turned the corner and there they stood.

This time, there were fewer pedestrians on the street and the men were closer—too far away for a conversation, but well within shouting distance. They just stood and watched her. This time the Maypole was holding the boy's hand more tightly.

They're trying to intimidate me, she thought. *They're trying to scare me. I'll show them that I'm not a pushover.*

"What do you want?" she called out. "How is Pisti?"

She stood up straight and tall and marched in their direction.

"What is it? What do you want?"

As she got closer, the men suddenly broke eye contact, turned, and hurried off. The boy kept looking back at her. He looked like he was warning her not to follow.

Elza fumed all day after that. She crashed pots and pans and cleaved meat in two with heavy-handed swipes. She still felt bad about the incident, but to threaten her! To threaten her after she had spent so much time worrying and looking for them, after she had even been assaulted. It was too much. She wouldn't stand for it.

At lunch time she went into the dining room and looked out the picture window again. No sign of them. The Motorcycle Officer was eating a cold sour-cherry soup. She sat down at his table.

"I never thanked you for that night with the boys," she said.

The officer put his spoon down and looked quizzically at her. "What? You mean with those Gypsies?" he said. "It was nothing. An accident."

"I've felt horrible about it ever since," she said. "I went to their quarter looking for them."

The Motorcycle Officer was incredulous. "Why did you go there?"

"Because it was wrong. I wanted to apologize."

"It was an accident! No need to make any more out of it."

"But I hit him," Elza insisted, "and he's not my child."

The officer huffed and shook his head. "They deserved it."

"I'd really hate to harm *anybody*," Elza said. "Anyway, I wanted to thank you for looking out for me, all the same."

"No worries," he said. "Consider it my pleasure." He spooned some sour-cherry soup into his mouth and wiped away a drop from his chin. "I like these lunches you're serving!" he began again. "It reminds me of when I was in training. There was an officer's club right across from the academy. It feels like food from those times."

Elza knew what he was talking about, and she smiled at him. In the old days there had been home-style restaurants all around the city, places where decent-sized meals could feed workers with subsidized food. One didn't see them anymore.

"Thanks," she said. "I'm just hoping to stay in business."

It was dark out again before she left the restaurant. She checked outside the big picture window to see if anyone was there. When she was sure the coast was clear, she walked out. She turned back to lock the door and suddenly, the men were standing beside her. She tried to stay calm. She just wanted to get this over with.

"Where is Pisti?" she asked impatiently. "Is he well?"

The Maypole said nothing. Up close, she noticed he had droopy eyelids. He looked at her without expression. The rounder one reached into his pocket and pulled out a stack of photographs.

"Ah," he said. His voice was hot and sugary. She felt it sticking to her. "Lookit, we're not trying to frighten you. We hope we didn't. We've been unsure of how to approach you. And then we heard *you* were looking for *us*! Thank you so much. We have been in Budapest. Little Pisti was hurt very badly in the fall, you see. Very badly. We took them all to our village the night of the accident, but then he had a seizure and so we had to get him to hospital. Look."

Elza winced as they handed her the photographs. On top of the stack was Pisti, looking asleep or unconscious. His forehead had an ugly gash and he looked green. Elza almost cried at the sight of him. She flipped to the second picture with shaky hands. It was of a woman spooning Pisti food. She went through all of them—all photographs of Pisti with his family around him.

"He has been very sick because of this," his uncle said.

Elza felt a tear and wiped it away. She handed the pictures back.

"It was an accident," she said. "You must believe me that I wouldn't hurt a child this way."

The rounder uncle nodded. The Maypole sneered.

"Lookit, we know it was an accident," the uncle said. "His cousin told us everything. They were spanked for causing this mess."

She suddenly felt bad for the other two boys, as well.

"Is there anything I can do for him? Do you need any help?"

The uncle gave a start as if he were going to say something, but silenced himself. He looked at the Maypole.

"What is it?" Elza said. "Is it money? Do you need money?"

Both uncles raised their eyebrows.

"Well, lookit, I'm ashamed to ask," the rotund one said. "You already gave the Shopkeeper some, and we heard he belted you. My brother had a talk with him about that. I'd be ashamed to ask for more. But the truth is with all the traveling between the hospital in Budapest and my village, with all the provisions we have to take, and the pay we have to slip the doctors, we can't afford it. You know, we're Gypsies. They're not going to give our Pisti anything extra at the hospital unless we slip them some forints. So, you know, three thousand for the train tickets for each aunt. Three thousand for food for the week. Ten thousand for the doctor whenever we see him. It adds up, miss."

Elza had nothing on her to give them just then, but she had an idea and she unlocked the door.

"Come inside," she said.

The two men followed her in. She walked to the wall where the silver concave mirrors were hanging—had been hanging for years. There were six of them. She remembered they were expensive when she had bought them. She took two of them down with the Maypole's help.

"I'm sorry, but this is all I have right now. Why don't you see how much you can get for them. If you can use the rest, meet me tomorrow before I open and you can take them. See if this helps."

The short, fat uncle was beside himself with gratitude. He looked at Elza appreciatively.

"Are you sure about this, miss?" he asked. "They look expensive."

"Take them," she said. "May I come visit Pisti?"

The short one looked at the Maypole, who sighed heavily and shook his head.

"The women might not appreciate it. They've been after us to call the police on you. However, as you might imagine, we're not fond of police."

Elza opened her purse and found she had a two-thousand-forint note, after all.

"I understand," she said as she handed them the money. "Why don't you take this as well! The mirrors are easily eight thousand apiece. Maybe more."

The round uncle was effusive with appreciation. The tall one didn't seem to share his enthusiasm. Elza shook hands with both of them and told them to come by in the morning if they thought they could use the others.

"I'm sure we can. I'm sure we can use them. Thank you so much!"

"Please tell Pisti I'm very sorry," Elza said. "Please tell him I want him to get better and that I hope to hear from him soon."

The round uncle nodded at her.

"Just as soon as he's better," he said.

Fifteen

Elza took the remaining mirrors from her wall the next morning. She figured she could clean them and have them ready for the men if they were needed. Though she was relieved to finally have an explanation for the family's disappearance, and to be able to help them in some way, she did not want to have to spend any more time with them than was necessary. In fact, when she was finished cleaning the mirrors, she placed them just beside the entrance in anticipation of their arrival. Should the men knock or peek in, should they visit her and ask for them, she could hand them over straightaway without having to invite them in.

She noticed that her wall seemed smaller and barren now without the mirrors; the discolored oval outlines made the restaurant appear drab and even a little dingy. Everything seemed older somehow. She looked at the dining room and thought about Dora's and the Sous-Chef's restaurant going up. She would have to repaint, she thought. She would have to redecorate completely.

For a moment she let her mind drift to colors and accents. Then came a sudden knock on the glass of the picture window. The uncles had returned. They were smoking cigarettes and looking in. The Round Man was waving at her, beckoning her to the door. His meaty little fingers were clasped around his cane. Elza walked in his direction and unlocked it. She stuck her head out.

"Good morning," he said loudly and just as sweetly as he had the evening before, as though he were an old friend. "Lookit, I think we can use those mirrors you promised. We were able to sell the ones you gave us to a friend. He liked them very much. We didn't get as much as you said, but we think if we sell him the rest, then that should definitely cover things for Pisti, for a while, we think. Can we still have them? Would you mind?"

He smiled. Elza didn't return it. She felt clearly now that she was being taken in, but her sense of guilt still nagged at her.

"Just a moment," she said.

She bent down and picked up the mirrors, handing them out the door to the Maypole one by one until he held a stack in his arms. When she had finished, she moved to close the door on them again, but the Round Man was able to jam his cane in its hinges. The door bounced back open.

"I'm ashamed to ask," he said confidently, stepping fully into her restaurant. "But would you happen to have one more? Just to be sure? I'm afraid of heading all the way to Budapest only to discover once we've reached the hospital that we're still short a few forints. They'd send us away right when we needed to be there most, right when being there might make all the difference. I know a few forints isn't much, miss, but we're not able to work these days. We had the job at the zoo, but they let us go when we missed too many hours because of all the hospital visits. Anything else you might have would be helpful. Any trifle. I'm sure there's something here you wouldn't miss."

Elza stifled a scoff. She was growing angry. His sugary voice couldn't veil the fact that his eyes roved hungrily over every inch of her and over every corner of her dining room. She could see the adding machine in his brain tallying up the contents of the restaurant. She watched as his eyes lingered over her chairs, as his lips became wet when he counted them silently. He could not conceal his avarice. Not one bit. It was crass. Repugnant. But she was too emotionally drained to fight it. She just wanted them to leave.

She looked around the dining room and took it all in herself. Surely there *was* something she could give them that would satisfy them.

"Do you think you can use candles?" she asked. "What about the candlestick holders?"

A broad smile cracked open like a fault line along the Round Man's face. He licked his lips hungrily and stroked the stubble on his chin.

"Why, just last week at the hospital, a visiting friend said he needed a few for his daughter's wedding. I think we can sell them to him."

Elza sighed and stepped aside to allow them to walk in farther. Yes, they were repugnant, but they were Pisti's guardians, and she was the one who had put him in a hospital bed.

"Take them," she said. "They're yours."

The men spilled into the dining room as messily as a tipped-over wineglass. They enthusiastically ransacked the place, scurrying around her tables and grabbing up the candles and their brass holders. The Maypole was carrying the mirrors, and the Round Man was stuffing both his own and his brother's pockets with the rest of the loot. When not all of the candlesticks would fit, he turned back to Elza.

"Would you have a bag or box that I can carry these in? I'm ashamed to ask."

And now I'm even helping them rob me! Elza thought to herself. *I guess we all deserve one another.*

Elza went into the kitchen anyway and came out with a box the onions had come in. She handed it to the Round Man and he filled it in a matter of seconds. They examined their booty as they made their way to the door. Elza held it open for them. The Round Man took one last look back.

"I like the cuckoo clock," he said hopefully. "Do you need it?"

Elza shook her head.

"I do, in fact," she said coolly.

He smiled sheepishly.

"Yes, well. This should certainly cover everything," he said. "I can't imagine how it couldn't. You never know with these doctors, though. They come up with all sorts of things. Always something new. Something more expensive."

Elza didn't respond. She shut the door behind them and watched them walk away. They passed the Postal Inspector on the street, who eyed them suspiciously. He knocked at the restaurant door.

"Everything all right here?" he asked. "Are you open?" He reached for her mail and presented it to her.

Elza invited him in. She took the postcard he handed.

"Redecorating," she explained as he looked around the ransacked room in stunned silence.

"Looks different in the morning," he remarked. "I thought maybe you were open for breakfast. I was going to order something. Do you even make breakfast?"

Elza nodded absently. She was examining the front of the postcard. It was from the lake country, a picture of Lake Balaton. The professors had sent it. She looked at the Postal Inspector and shook her head.

"What did you say? Breakfast?" she asked.

"Yes," he said. "I'm so hungry. I hurried out and left without a bite to eat this morning. I have a few minutes to myself. Are you open?"

Elza thought about what she had in the larder. Cooking anything might actually make her feel better just now.

"I can make you eggs." she offered. "Something simple along with a cup of coffee and a salted roll. Would you like that?"

"Sounds good," said the Postal Inspector. "You don't mind?"

"Of course not," she said. "Sit. It'll be a moment. I only have to brew some coffee and get the ingredients together."

In the empty kitchen, Elza was able to read the postcard more closely. The Critic was having a good time, the professors wrote. They had all visited the culinary institute together and were now spending their days lakeside. His visit had lasted nearly a month already, and it turned out that he was an excellent badminton player and had even won a tournament. He was pleased with his stay and in much better spirits. And then this: They were coming back to Delibab. They would return in time for the flower carnival.

Elza's mind buzzed as she prepared the coffee and grabbed three eggs. She was distracted when she cut several fatty slices of bacon into a frying pan and they began to melt and sizzle. She threw in fresh onions rings and a handful of diced sausage on top. She cracked open the eggs and gently whisked them in a bowl along with a pinch of salt, pepper, and paprika. And when the meat in the pan looked crisp enough, she carefully poured the egg mixture over it and lowered the flame underneath. The entire time she was thinking about the Critic, about whether or not she would make another attempt to cook for him, and if she did, what she might make and how she would execute it. When the eggs thickened and were nearly cooked through, she sprinkled some freshly cut parsley and a diced hot green pepper over the top. They sank a little on the pool of egg and made it more colorful, but Elza was barely conscious of this. She had not realized what she had created, not even while she was sliding it onto a plate along with the salted roll. She carried it to the dining room with a steaming cup of coffee.

"What are you two doing here?"

Her friend Eva and the Motorcycle Officer were now sitting at their own tables. She placed the plate of food down in front of the Postal Inspector. She saw that she had left the door to the restaurant propped open.

"That smells delicious," the Postal Inspector said.

The Motorcycle Officer peeked over at his food. He moved over to the Postal Inspector's table.

"If you don't mind, I'll have one of those as well," he said. "Could you hold the hot peppers? I have an ulcer."

"I'll just have some buttered toast and coffee, dear," her friend Eva said. "Or a braided raisin bread, if you have it. Why are you waiting tables, by the way? Where are your waiters?"

Elza tried to protest. She explained that it was all a misunderstanding, that she wasn't *really* serving breakfast, when a young man, a foreigner carrying a backpack, stuck his head in the door.

"Food?" he asked Elza haltingly.

They were all staring at her now. For the first time Elza looked at the plate she had prepared, and she watched as the Postal Inspector dug in. She knew exactly how many eggs she had left. She remembered a couple of loaves of day-old bread.

The young man was still waiting in the doorway.

"It seems I am making breakfast," she said. She beckoned him in. "Only a couple of things on the menu, though."

The student turned, stepped out of the restaurant, and called out. A group of straggly-looking foreigners paraded up the sidewalk. Elza held the door open for them as they piled in. They chattered in a Scandinavian language and pointed at the Postal Inspector's plate.

Elza returned to the kitchen. She took out a second pan and started preparing omelets two at a time, but she also thought of slicing the loaf of bread into thick slices and covering them in the leftover beaten egg in order to prepare a second meal, a savory, egg-coated bread. It turned out this was a good idea because by the time she exited carrying the omelet plates on her arms, three more customers had arrived.

The Postal Inspector was the first to finish and he left a few wrinkled bank notes on the table. The Motorcycle Officer did the same when he walked out. Eva lingered longer and eventually began helping Elza with serving coffee and rolls.

"What fun!" she kept announcing. "What fun! But why aren't your waiters here? How much are you going to charge for this? It's a brilliant idea, Elza. There's no place to get a decent breakfast in this town."

Elza looked around. Yes, a breakfast place, she thought. Breakfast and lunch only. Less overhead and no encroaching competition. She could scratch her way back to an evening restaurant in time. Why not?

She and Eva served the foreigners and everyone else who wandered in for hours until the eggs ran out. There were a surprising number of people looking for breakfast. Elza asked herself why she had never thought of it before. Finally, as the last breakfast was being eaten, Elza's line cooks and waiters arrived to prepare for the lunch service. They saw the mess and Elza explained that she was going to be changing a few things.

It took them all a moment to warm up to the idea of so much work in the morning, but in the end they agreed to go along.

She sent a waiter to the market to replenish the food that had been eaten while the line cooks began preparing the day's soup. Elza and Eva cleared the dishes from the tables and began washing up.

"This was so much fun," Eva said. "Maybe I'll come by to help every morning. I've always been an early riser anyway. It'll give me something to do. But we have to paint those walls right away. We can look for colors together.

"That would be nice," Elza said. "Thank you."

The Postal Inspector told his colleagues at the post office about the changes at Tulip. The Motorcycle Officer told his colleagues at the police station. Eva told everyone at her hairdresser's, and so it only took a matter of days before locals buzzed about the changes at their once-favorite restaurant and the spectacular breakfasts being served there. Curious, the same people returned—the same fat walruses and their same ostrich-sized wives. They sat and ordered the savory coated bread. They drank coffee while reading the morning headlines. They didn't linger like they did in the evening. They ate purposefully and set out in a quarter of the time. Tables turned over at a faster pace.

Another group of foreigners ordered eggs and coffee and were talking loudly in the restaurant. They came from the local hostel. The Scandinavian trekkers who had come in that first day had returned to their hostel and posted Tulip's information on a bulletin board. The owner of the hostel had read the positive review and called Elza. He explained that he was trying to find places that would offer a discount for his guests, and when she agreed, he directed everyone who visited him back to her restaurant for breakfast and lunch.

In a few days Elza grew accustomed to the rhythm of a morning eatery and figured out what she needed. She saw, for example, that men seemed to like her heartier meals. They were the ones who ate the most sausage and eggs. She went through several hundred eggs a day supplying them with omelets. They devoured them and twisted their napkins ferociously before setting out. Women, on the other hand, drank a lot more coffee and ordered more of the braided bread or toast and jam. Elza tried to keep things simple, but she did have one experimental breakfast she'd invented, a mixture of cornmeal, fried onions, and bacon slices. She noticed that the adventurous tourists ordered that one.

This was a good idea Elza had stumbled upon, thanks to the Postal Inspector. She had to admit it to herself. And it energized her. Once she began the breakfast service, she awoke not with the sense of dread she had been accustomed to lately, but with a little bit of hope and purpose. She found that she was soon rising from sleep earlier than she had before. In fact, she was up at sunrise, dressed and out in the cool morning air by the time the first tram arrived. She took a stroll to the market before heading to the restaurant and she bought honey or fresh cottage cheese, or eggs, and green onions. For the first time in a very long while, her anxieties quieted.

Sixteen

A week before the flower carnival began, during what were certainly the hottest days of summer, a staging tent was erected behind the railyards of the Delibab train station. Blocks of ice and industrial fans were set up to keep it cool. It was a tall structure, visible from the platforms, as tall as the station itself, with streamers blowing from its spires and space enough inside to shade several hundred people or—as was presently the case—to house twelve floats as they were prepared and decorated entirely with fresh flower blooms and rubber cement.

Enthusiastic hobby gardeners and groundskeepers from the city's botanical garden diligently followed schematics and transformed each of the floats into one of a myriad of chicken-wire replicas—everything from pastoral scenes of bounding deer to the colossal pyramids of Giza; from local landmark buildings like the great church outside of Elza's flat to an Arabian oasis, to the whale Moby Dick. All of these floats had been decided upon by their sponsors, and they had been designed months earlier. Now, they were being painstakingly arranged a single bloom at a time, a shock of colored carnations here, a wall of roses there, hyacinth above, narcissus gathered and set below, and baby's breath for the spaces in between or to serve as general ground-cover. In fact, there was so much baby's breath on the floats, there were so many varieties of blooms being arranged, and there were so many open cans of rubber cement lying around, that as they did every year, in order to avoid a repeat of the great tragedy of 1983—when an asthmatic had died while working on the float for *Grease*—the city hospital had put an allergist on call and arranged for beds to be available should someone succumb to the overabundance of fragrances wafting throughout the enclosed area.

The manner of creating these floats, though intricate, was simple, really. First, a diagram of the float was drawn. Then, a platform was built over a vehicle and twisted chicken-wire frames of the intended character or building were built and attached to the platform. These wire models served as the substructure upon which the flowers would be attached. Finally, the flowers were laid atop and beside one another one blossom at a time; they were threaded through the wire mesh and either held fast with string or pasted on with rubber cement until an entire scene was built.

Needless to say, the amount of flowers needed for this endeavor reached very near several tons! And as Delibab wasn't, say, Ecuador or Kenya, where the growing season in the mountains lasts for months; and as a lot of these flowers had to be shipped in via special delivery, a supply line of diesel trucks rattled in from Budapest, their covered beds full of flowers. The delivery was coordinated by the finest civic planners and logistical minds. Truck drivers pushed themselves heroically and drove grueling overnight shifts to arrive in time, but their efforts were rewarded. They were paid handsomely and were invited to stay for the carnival, which was legendary—not only because of the amazing flower floats, but also because of the lean-legged daughters of the city and surrounding countryside who marched between them as majorettes.

As they pulled up to the back of the tent and dropped off their deliveries, they kept an eye on the practicing girls. The young women practiced their twirling and choreography cheerfully in a nearby meadow. They threw their batons in the air, spun around completely, and wiggled their bottoms before catching the batons behind their backs. They kicked and twirled with military precision, and the truck drivers shook their heads in amazement. It was summer, and they loved parades. Loved everything about them. Loved the sound of the marching bands and beating drums. Loved how happy and rosy the young women were. Loved how the girls flashed smiles that would melt the hardest heart.

Dora's father had hired three of these girls, all redheads, to ride the float he was sponsoring for the Three Roses. Wire frames had been built of cream puffs, pies, and cinnamon rolls. Two wire-mesh children stood front and center. On the stern of the float was a dais topped by a white chair that would seat a charioteer. Directly behind this chair, rising up from what would be a bed of baby's breath, was the wire frame for three wild roses, each one six feet long! The lateral roses were placed at an angle. The center one stood straight up behind the chair. It looked like a throne.

The workers were finishing the construction by using white and yellow carnations as pastry cream. They used wild roses to form the three giant roses behind the chair. They filled the spaces with colored carnations. The children's hair was made of yellow narcissus blooms. A sign on the side of the float announced the restaurant's name in stark red paint. Dora's father was pleased with his design, and he couldn't wait for Dora and the Sous-Chef to see it.

"Look at those pyramids!" the Sous-Chef cried as they entered the tent. He was growing ever more excited about the parade and their opening day. He raced among the floats and called them out to Dora. "And here's Moby Dick! And there is an oasis! And here is ours!"

He led Dora to their float and they looked up at it with her father. The Sous-Chef whistled.

"Now this is really something," he said. "Children and pies."

"Who's going to sit there?" Dora asked her father, pointing at the chair on the dais.

"I think you should!" said the Sous-Chef. "You can wave to the crowds. I'll keep the kitchen running and make sure the street vendors are fully stocked with Linzer cookies."

"Yes, yes," Dora's father said. "You and your mother can take turns waving at the crowd and handing treats out to the children. The majorettes will help you."

Dora looked at the float. She would have preferred to be at the opening of her restaurant, but she understood the need for marketing and knew there was no one better for it.

She squeezed the Sous Chef's hand. "I'll head back to the restaurant just as soon as the parade is over to give you a break."

For now, they both went back to the restaurant. People were stopping by at all hours to say hello or to get a peek. All of Dora's father's business associates had been by. They had shaken the Sous-Chef's hand and congratulated him on his certain success. They had congratulated the couple on their upcoming marriage and wished them years of happiness. It was a wonder at times that they were able to get anything done at all with the constant visits they were receiving.

"If this is any indication of our opening day," the Sous-Chef said, "then we are going to be busy. Everything has to work perfectly."

Dora agreed and the couple worked as hard as they were able.

Seventeen

Elza and Eva repainted the dining room at Tulip a sunny yellow. They put up new curtains. They removed the linens from the tables and stored them away in the office, leaving the warm wood exposed. Elza put new paper placemats down, but she kept the same linen napkins. She knew she would always need those.

After the painting had been finished, she and Eva sat at a table, drinking coffee.

"It looks like a different restaurant entirely," Eva said.

"It does," Elza said. "I don't even miss the mirrors."

New menus for breakfast and lunch service were printed. Elza continued to keep things as simple as she had on that first day. There were stock items for both meals: a savory egg-coated bread and omelets for breakfast, Chicken Paprika and stuffed cabbage for lunch. She bought a small sandwich board and put that out front with the day's specials listed—whatever was fresh and in season.

Since breakfast had been added and word had spread, business had picked up considerably. The Dishwasher had brought his nephew in as he had said he would, and once the young man started working he proved to be as efficient in the kitchen as his uncle, not to mention cheaper. It really was a win.

Eva came to help every morning as she had said she would and finally decided to accept a little pay. They soon discovered that she was an even better hostess than Elza ever had been; Elza listened from the kitchen with a smile while Eva cooed and laughed with the male customers.

"I could get married every week here," she whispered to Elza on her way to drop off dirty dishes. "It's a goldmine! How have you managed to stay single so long? It's going to be impossible for me to keep their names straight."

Elza shook her head. "No, thank you," she said. "I just couldn't see getting married again."

Eva shrugged. "Suit yourself," she said. "More for me."

When the flower tent went up and it was only a few days before the carnival, Elza made her own trip to procure flowers. She wanted several bunches of tulips for the restaurant. But there was a premium on the price of flowers, and the truck driver she asked insisted there were none to spare; they had been carefully inventoried and were expected at the pyramids of Giza.

"I only need a few bunches," Elza pleaded. "Every shop owner in the city will have flowers in their windows. I only need a few bunches of the yellow tulips."

The truck driver fiddled with a key chain and looked at the flower pallets.

"I suppose a couple of bunches won't hurt," he said.

"Of course not," Elza responded. "They won't even miss them. Thank you so much."

She took the tulips in her arms and tried to make her way back to the restaurant. The authorities had closed the promenade, however, to set up stands and benches and to arrange rest stops and tents. They had set up detours for pedestrians to follow. Elza cursed under her breath. Soon, she realized the detour was leading her right past little Pisti's cottage in the Roma quarter.

She wondered if the candlesticks had helped the family or if they had been able to get a good price for the mirrors.

"I might as well," she said under her breath, and went up to the familiar gate. But the cottage again looked desolate.

She steeled herself and walked to the store on the corner.

A new bell above the door jingled when she pushed it open, and the Shopkeeper looked up from silverware he was polishing. He rolled his eyes and audibly sighed when he saw her. The shop seemed different. She realized two of her mirrors were hanging on the walls.

"Where did you get these candlesticks?" she asked, spotting them on a shelf with other bric-a-brac.

The Shopkeeper looked in the same direction. He put down a silver fork he was polishing.

"Our friends!" he announced. "Our dear friends brought a bunch of old stuff in here a few weeks ago wanting to make a deal. They brought in nearly twenty of these things and a handful of mirrors." He gestured at the mirror on the wall behind him.

"These are mine," she said. "And that's my mirror!"

The Shopkeeper made a show of examining his fork.

"Well, I bought them," he said, finally. "They're not too expensive, if you're interested in buying them back. I'll make you a deal. I have more than I can use. The others are in the back collecting dust."

"No, thank you," she said. "I'm not interested.

"So, what do you want?" he asked.

Elza fiddled with a candlestick.

"I'm still looking for them," she said. "I gave them this stuff, and they said they'd use the money to help their little nephew."

The Shopkeeper put his hands up in a gesture of exasperation.

"Lady," he said. "Look. Those people don't work like you or me. They just don't. They moved away ages ago. If they ever come back it'll probably be to the other side of the city. So, like I told you before, whatever you think you owe them, you don't. Give it up. It's a game for them. They're just gone. Why not get on with your life and quit coming around here?"

The Shopkeeper returned to rubbing a spoon aggressively. Elza walked out. She wouldn't come back here again.

Eighteen

On the day of the flower carnival, Elza awoke with the tolling of the church bells at six A.M. She dressed quickly in clothing she had laid out the evening before and, impatient with the elevator, bounded down the stairs of her building. As she hurried to the restaurant she thought about the busy morning she would have and the money to be made. Today could provide a windfall that would help her back into dinner service.

All of her employees arrived on time and began vigorously prepping ingredients for breakfast or cleaning the dining room. When Eva arrived, Elza met her at the door with the new dishwasher and sent them both out to pass out billets to the growing crowd of people in the Centrum. Though tram service was interrupted until the afternoon, a few people, tourists, Elza imagined, were already milling around looking for something to do. Since little else would be open for a few more hours, Elza knew they would have no problem handing out the billets—coupons for a reduced-rate breakfast, with directions to the restaurant on the back.

"What a clever idea," Eva said when she read the slip of paper. She looked at the new dishwasher. "Let's make sure to hand them out to large families and big crowds first."

Elza remained behind at the restaurant to tend to the meat that had been marinating. She had marinated strips of pork loin in white wine overnight after her old professors had called her to say they were back in town, the Critic still in tow. Elza had invited them to Tulip for breakfast or lunch—whichever they preferred—and they had agreed to come later in the morning. Afterward, Elza would leave with them to watch the parade at its end, at the Great Park outside of the Centrum.

Elza thought about them as she inspected the pork loin. She considered going over to the hotel and checking on them, but then decided against it.

Eva and the new dishwasher passed all the fliers around and returned to the restaurant just in time to open. There was already a crowd of regulars waiting at the door, and a growing group of new customers stood in line too, with fliers in their hands. Elza was standing just inside and said good morning to each customer.

"Come have breakfast," she said.

One of her line cooks carried out the sandwich board with the day's specials, both of them pork dishes. A bacon omelet for breakfast and a seared paprika dill pork loin for lunch. Should the professors and the Critic arrive, this time she would have their meals ready herself. No fanfare. Only a special of the day.

By 8:15 A.M. Elza was in the kitchen cooking with her line cooks and Tulip was full. She could hear the rattle of plates and the dinging of silverware against crockery. Breakfast was a much louder affair than dinner. She had noticed that right away. The work was also a lot faster. The Headwaiter seemed like a yo-yo bouncing in and out of the kitchen, shouting new orders, handing over tickets, shouting for quicker service.

"It's a madhouse!" he cried.

As people continued to arrive at the Centrum looking for a spot along the parade route, they heard about the restaurant from the early birds who had returned to the promenade with full bellies and big smiles that prompted others to ask what they were so happy about.

"There's a restaurant around the corner serving good breakfast."

Some paradegoers pulled out the salted rolls they had packed and sighed at the sight of them. They had gone moist. The parade would not start for another couple of hours. The only other things open on the promenade were the fast-food restaurants and a few kiosks selling newspapers. They looked up at the Three Roses and, though there were people inside preparing, and it looked promising through the window, it was also closed. They shrugged.

"Not much else to do," they reasoned. "Let's go and check out the place on the billet we were given."

By nine A.M. there was a long line outside of the restaurant. Elza and her crew put their heads down and plowed away at clearing the orders. Eva was still gracious and flirty, but she made sure the waiters turned their tables over as quickly as they could. She helped clear tables and directed foot traffic.

"No lingering this morning," she told them. "Turn it over! If they finish their breakfast, let them have a moment to finish their coffee. If they don't look like they'll order anything else, take them their checks whether they ask or not."

She had succeeded in keeping the line moving quickly enough to keep the growing crowd at ease. This, plus the look of bliss people in the line recognized on the faces of the people walking out, were enough to keep the crowd standing where they were.

"Must be good stuff," one said.

"Must be."

The atmosphere had taken on the quality of a fair. When a street musician walked by on his way to set up on the promenade, people called out to him to stop and play his violin. He agreed, and they listened and threw change in his case every time he finished another song.

The line soon caused stirring on the promenade. Once it had snaked around the corner and up the street toward the hotel, people on the promenade saw the tail end of it and thought it was something related to the carnival. They went to investigate. The Maypole and his brother were among the curious crowd. They were back in town for the carnival as well, aimlessly wandering the streets, when they saw the line and began to follow it. They were surprised to see that it began right at the door of Elza's restaurant. The Round Man slapped his brother's back in astonishment.

"Lookit!" he said. "Look how well our little friend is doing. Perhaps we should pay her a visit and ask her to help our Pisti. He could use a hand, don't you agree?"

The Maypole nodded. The brothers marched directly to the front of the line and tried to walk into the restaurant.

"Hey! What do you two think you're doing?" a voice called out. "No cutting. Wait your turn. The line is moving fast enough."

The tall uncle turned and sneered. The round uncle put his hands up.

"We're not going in to eat. We just want to say hello to a friend who works in the kitchen."

He stuck his head in the door and saw Eva. She was directing a waiter to a table. When she spotted him she squinted at him coldly, but he beckoned to her anyway.

"Yes," she said. "Can I help you?"

"Hello," the Round Man said in his sweet voice. "I was looking for the nice lady who owns the restaurant. The dark-haired chef. We're friends of hers. Can you tell her that Pisti's uncles are outside."

Eva was suspicious. She wondered how Elza could know these men.

"She's terribly busy right now," she said. "As you can see we're all a bit busy. Can you come back later?"

The Maypole pushed her aside and walked into the restaurant. He stood at least three heads above her. He headed for the kitchen door. Eva tried to stop him, but he pushed her aside again and walked into the kitchen. The Round Man followed, smiling and waving to uneasy customers.

"Just visiting a friend in the kitchen," he said. "Please don't let us disturb you."

"You can't go in there," she said. "You can't."

Elza was at her station. She had not looked up, but was whisking a bowl of eggs and was about to pour them into a steaming pan.

"Elza," Eva called out frantically. "I tried to stop them!"

Elza looked up and her face fell when she saw the uncles. What nerve, she thought. She was glad a knife was in reach.

"What do you want?" she asked.

The brothers approached on either side of her. The Round Man pointed at the pan.

"Do all of those people out there know they are standing in line just for eggs?"

Elza looked at the pan and threw in a handful of sliced mushrooms.

"What do you want?" she asked again impatiently. "I'm a little busy."

"It's Pisti," he said. "He's taken a turn for the worse. We need money for a specialist from Prague."

"Oh, do you, now," Elza said. "Deathly ill, is he?"

She folded the omelet in half.

"I'm calling the police," Eva announced. She turned to go into Elza's office, but Elza called her back.

"It's fine," she said. "I'll explain everything later." She turned to the brothers.

"You know that cuckoo clock you like so much?" she said. 'It's in my office. You may have it. But I won't give you anything else until you bring Pisti to see me."

The Round Man shook his head and laughed.

"What can we do with a cuckoo clock?" he asked. "I imagine you're making really good cash this morning. Can't you spare a few notes? Pisti is worse now than he was last time we visited. He can't travel. A cuckoo clock isn't going to help us now. You think because we're Gypsies we'll take whatever you are throwing away. We're not simple."

Elza was done. She placed the omelet on a plate and looked them each in the eye. "I'm not giving you anything else but that damned cuckoo clock," she said. "And that's the last thing you get until I see him. Take it or leave it, but go now or we will call the police."

The Maypole glowered at her. He took a step at her as though he might strike her. Elza didn't wither, but reached instead for her butcher's knife. Everyone else in the kitchen stopped what they were doing. The line cooks came over from their station. The Dishwasher's nephew emerged from behind a stack of plates. They each brandished whatever cutlery was on hand, like a band of kitchen pirates. The round brother held his taller one back.

"A misunderstanding," he announced to the room. "We can come back later when you're less stressed."

"If you come back, it had better be with the child," Elza said. "Otherwise, I'm calling the police as soon as I see you standing at my door."

The brothers turned and hustled themselves out of the restaurant.

"I think this cow is dry," the Maypole said.

"I think you're right there," the Round Man replied. "Not too shabby, though. Not shabby at all, I'd say."

Nineteen

Elza tried to put the visit behind her while the morning rush raged on.

Things were just slowing down and the lunch orders were beginning to trickle in when the kitchen door burst open again and Eva came walking in hurriedly. This time, though, she was practically beaming.

"They're here! Your professors and that critic are sitting in the dining room. They're commenting on the changes. I seated them and sent a waiter over, but they've only ordered coffees. Should I do something? Do you want to send them something from the kitchen?"

Elza shook her head. She worried about the light order, but she would not force anything on them. She turned to her line cooks and asked if they could handle the last hour on their own.

"It's slowed down enough," they answered. "We'll be fine."

Elza finished her last batch of omelets and set them out for a waiter to deliver. She left her station and washed her hands and face at a nearby sink. It had been a long morning, and she was sweaty and stewing and didn't feel particularly friendly, but she realized there was nothing she could do about that save get over it. *I have what I have*, she thought to herself. She went to her office for a moment's rest. She gave her visitors a good ten minutes to settle and order before she went to the dining room.

The men were talking animatedly and reading her new menu.

"Elza!" the Professor of Sauces exclaimed when he saw her approach. The Professor of Meats and the Critic stood up.

"Elza, my dear," said the Professor of Meats. "You remember our friend from *Le Gourmand*, yes? He's back and in much better spirits!"

Elza shook the Critic's hand.

"I heard you have been enjoying your holiday," she said.

The Critic smiled and placed his hands on the table. If she was not mistaken, he seemed to have lost a kilo or two from around his waist. The shirt he wore seemed looser than the one he had worn the night they met.

"I have had a marvelous time here!" he said. "These two have been fine hosts. Lake Balaton was lovely. I even won a badminton competition! And the food has been wonderful. I'm sorry to be leaving soon, but I'll be coming back in a couple of months."

"I'm glad it wasn't a wasted trip for you then," Elza said.

"Not at all. Not at all," the Critic answered. "I feel like I made new friends and put a lot of things into perspective."

Elza didn't answer, but she knew just what he meant. She had also put things into perspective. She sat at the table, and all the men made an effort to hold her chair for her. They still only had three cups of coffee in front of them. Had they ordered anything at all? She looked over at Eva, who furtively shook her head. Elza decided to give it one last try.

"But you must try something," she announced. "I've changed everything, as you can see. It's nearly noon. Aren't you hungry?"

The men looked at one another and waved their hands.

"I couldn't eat another bite," the Critic said.

He said it innocently enough, but the two professors looked as though they had been caught using old mustard seeds in a dressing, or using duck eggs in a pastry. The Critic began reading her menu again.

"Elza, dear," the Professor of Sauces explained. "I'm so embarrassed. We ate at the new restaurant on the promenade. It was their opening day. They had people at the hotel showing menus, and they offered all guests half-price entrées. The menu looked so inviting we thought we'd give it a peek. The meal was quite good, and we couldn't resist the pastries and dessert. I hope you're not disappointed."

The Critic looked up from the menu and nodded in agreement. "That one on the promenade," he said. "Three Roses? I have to say, it was a very creative selection of entrées." He put Elza's menu down and pushed it away. He picked up his coffee and sipped it. "And those desserts! Especially their marzipan cake. An entire cake made of marzipan! I was thinking I might cover it for the magazine. I have a bit of a sweet tooth, truth be told."

"I like how you've changed the restaurant," the Professor of Meats said, changing the subject when he noticed that Elza was not smiling.

"Yes," said the Critic, looking around as well. "It looks like you've been busy this month. A new menu. New selections. What's been happening?"

"I must say that I think a morning bistro is a fabulous idea," the Professor of Meats slapped the table and said when she didn't answer the Critic's question. "It's so hard to find a decent breakfast. I'll definitely be coming in tomorrow to have a taste. Or maybe I'll come for lunch. I'll decide tomorrow, but I guarantee you'll see me here."

Elza looked around her restaurant. Even with the fresh paint, it looked old-fashioned. It was certainly not worthy of the Silver Ladle. What had she been thinking? But she looked at a table with customers still eating and enjoying themselves. She should be enjoying herself too, she thought. Enjoying the fact that she had as much as she did. And it was a lot.

"If you like their restaurant so much then you *should* profile it," she said to the Critic, surprising them both.

The professors shifted uncomfortably in their seats and the Critic did not answer straightaway. He looked into his coffee, realizing he had been insensitive. "I imagine it must be hard for you to hear something like that," he finally said. "I know how hard you worked to get me here and how hard you work here every day. But they have quite a good restaurant."

Elza was nodding at him. She would be fine. After all, he had come all this way. He should cover something. She would still read his column, and then she would have the pleasure of knowing how she had made it all possible.

The Professor of Meats rose from the table. He looked at his watch.

"Shall we go?" he said. "We have a parade to catch. Can we steal you away from here, Elza?"

"Certainly," Elza said. "We should get moving."

Twenty

The Great Park outside the Centrum had pebbled paths for walking and an extensive lawn for sunbathing. There were forested areas near the zoo, where children liked to roam, and there was also a lake at the park's center where people rode the water slide, rented pedal boats, or skipped stones. Young children liked to throw bread to ducks and watch the backs of fish breaking the water's surface as the fish hunted insects. On the north end of the lake was the thermal bath that saw visitors all year round. The park was teeming with people on most days, especially during summer, but during the flower carnival the number of people at the park increased four-fold. They poured in from the streets. A market had sprung up with vendors selling food and folk art. The vendors stood around waiting for the parade to end and break apart. That's when they would make the most of their location—when the parade ended, and after the majorettes met their beaus and disappeared into the woods. The floats would be parked on the lawn for people to see up close. Stages were erected for performances. It was the boisterous culmination of a boisterous day.

And arriving at all the gaiety were Elza, her two professors, and the Critic. They had walked from the Centrum, and Elza had pointed out all the places the Critic should visit if he had time. She showed him the city museum, the newly refurbished villas that stood just outside the park, the thermal baths, and the university. In front of the university, which was also the entrance to the park, were a series of fountains. She showed him the statues of bathing women and they found an elevated place to stand. Elza felt completely relaxed. Neither she nor the Critic talked about restaurants or food. They seemed more like friends visiting after years apart.

"We'll wait here," she said to them. "The parade will come to us."

They lounged about. The Professor of Sauces left them to buy drinks and when he returned he handed them each a bottled mineral water and small, tidy-looking boxes of cookies.

"From the restaurant we ate at earlier," he said. "They have vendors all over the park selling Linzers. Very smart."

Elza opened her box. It contained strawberry Linzers. She took a bite and the cookie melted on her tongue. The strawberry filling tasted like perfectly ripe fruit and the cookie was buttery, with a hint of vanilla. The Critic was smiling at the box.

"I had a very dear friend," he whispered. "She loved Linzer cookies."

"Here. Take mine, too" she said.

The Critic took the box and thanked her.

They heard the sound of an approaching marching band. People stood up and surged toward the park's entrance. A large float came rolling up the main boulevard. It was the oasis. The crowd began clapping. The palm trees shook as the float rolled along, and that made the blooms shimmer; it looked like a mirage heading straight for them.

Parade goers swarmed the float as it came to a stop. The majorettes dropped their batons and broke rank, dispersing into the crowd.

An even louder drumming approached. It was a visiting samba troupe from Brazil. They beat the drums a little longer before the Brazilians also broke rank to become tourists. Then the next float approached decorated with children and pastries.

Dora and her mother were waving at the crowd and tossing marzipan roses out to the spectators. Children were running alongside them catching as many as they could. Dora wore her kitchen whites. Elza noticed that she had changed her eye shadow; her raccoon mask was gone, and she looked much more grown-up with a clean face, confident and hopeful.

Dora waved and threw roses into the crowd. No matter the competition, Elza thought, the trick was to stay in business. She'd lasted ten years. She knew she could continue for ten more. Perhaps Tulip wouldn't be as grandiose as the Three Roses, but it would do. For her.

The Critic dug the last Linzer cookie from his box. Elza touched his arm.

She pointed out to the lake at the pedal boats bobbing on the water. Right now there wasn't much of a line.

"Would you like to ride out on the lake with me?" she asked.

The Critic was hesitant. There was his weight to consider. He looked at the boats and then at Elza. She was certainly very pretty, he thought. How could he say no?

"Certainly," he said. "I'd like that."

"Would you like to come along?" she asked her old professors.

The two men shook their heads.

"No, no," said the Professor of Sauces. "We're too old for that and it's too hot. You two enjoy yourselves. We'll see you back at the hotel later."

Elza locked arms with the Critic and pulled him to the pedal boats. He insisted on renting the largest one, a four-seater swan with big plastic wheels and puddles on the seats. Elza stepped into the boat, and the Critic carefully held her arm to steady her. She wiped the puddles away as best she could with her hands and he followed.

"I haven't done anything like this since I was a kid," he said.

"Don't worry," Elza said. "I haven't either."

Seated, they began to pedal. Slowly at first, but then harder. Pedaling and laughing. In no time at all their swan had glided to the center of the lake. They were beginning to sweat and a breeze over the water cooled them off a bit. They stopped pedaling and let the swan drift. It was quieter on the lake, but they could still hear strains of music coming from the lawn. The Critic looked over at Elza shyly. He thought of his mother, and of Madame Isabelle. They would both approve of this, he thought. They might even be looking down at him and smiling. Here he was enjoying himself with an attractive woman. He opened the box she had given him earlier and offered her a cookie. She reached in and took it. She smiled at him.

"You know, I look forward to seeing your column every month," Elza said. "It's my favorite thing in the whole magazine. I drink a cup of coffee and imagine myself eating in the restaurant you've featured."

"It's an enjoyable job," the Critic said. "Most of the time. Sometimes, though, the chefs can be a little much."

"Really? How do you mean?"

The Critic caught himself. He remembered how he had come to be here. He looked at the dew over Elza's lip.

"Sometimes they have too many aspirations," he offered. "Nothing but aspirations. Hunger for all the wrong things when they should worry instead about getting their combinations right."

Elza put the cookie in her mouth and gazed at the shoreline. Aspirational chefs, she thought. Perhaps she had been one of them. But what now? What was she now?

Something on the shore caught her eye. She leaned forward to get a closer look.

"What is it?" the Critic asked. He had been considering whether to put his hand on her knee, but the look on her face now scared him off. "What do you see?"

Elza was squinting. She was leaning practically out of the boat. She gripped the handlebars so hard, her knuckles had gone white.

"Unbelievable," she said.

She began to pedal furiously. Her body shook from the strain. She grabbed his arm.

"Pedal!" she barked at him. "Pedal!"

The Critic tried. He pedaled furiously, but he could not keep up her pace and was soon winded. The boat started to drift into a circle.

"I can't pedal anymore," he said apologetically. "I can't. What's the matter? Did I say something wrong?"

Elza looked him dead in the eye. "Pedal! Pedal, or I'll jump in and swim."

The Critic was too chivalrous to allow her to do that. He imagined his mother being disappointed and Madame Isabelle shaking her head. He winced, but he grabbed onto the handlebar, took a breath, and pumped his legs up and down. The swan picked up its pace. He noticed that she hadn't let go of him. The Critic wondered at the sudden change that had overcome her. He had felt that she had been warming to him. *Maybe it was just my imagination,* he thought. He couldn't say one way or another. But her hand was still on his arm, and that was enough for him to decide to spend an extra day in Delibab.

"He's going to get away," she pleaded. "Please pedal harder."

He scanned the shore trying to determine who she was looking at. He wondered if it was an ex-lover . . . or maybe a current boyfriend. He scanned the shore again, wondering who his rival might be.

The pedal boat made its way even closer to shore.

When they were still a couple of meters away, Elza jumped off the boat and waded through the water.

"What are you doing?" the Critic called after her, now more puzzled than ever. "What is the matter?"

Elza was wading toward shore and pointing.

Now the Critic saw their quarry. Sitting with his back to them, in a larger group of street boys, was a child eating blue cotton candy.

"Pisti!" Elza shouted.

The boy turned, and the color left his face. He bolted like a rabbit, full-speed, into the woods.

"Pisti!" she called out again.

Pisti dodged left and right and made his way into the forest, with Elza chasing close behind him. A few people stopped to watch them pass.

"She's all wet," a woman remarked.

"They must have pushed her in the water and picked her pocket," her husband said.

"Watch out for pickpockets!" they announced.

The Critic abandoned the boat and lumbered after them.

"Elza," he called out to her. "What in the world?"

Pisti kept running, but Elza was closing in on him. The trees became more crowded and when the boy looked behind him, he tripped over an exposed root. Elza made a final stretch and got her hand on his shoulder before he hit the ground. Her fingers squeezed. She caught him! She turned him around to get a good look at him. He was perfectly fine.

A feeling of exultation ran through her. He was fine! Here he was right in front of her, and he was fine. His cheeks were covered in cotton candy.

"Pisti," she didn't mean to shout. She could see he was scared. She said it again more softly. She patted his head. "Pisti."

He put his hands in front of his face.

"Don't hit me, restaurant lady," he said.

"Pisti." She couldn't think of anything else to say. The shock had knocked all other thoughts out of her head. All she could think about was how healthy he looked.

"You're okay?" she said. "Are you all right?"

The Critic came wheezing up behind them now.

"It's the fat man!" Pisti shouted and was certain he was done for. "The fat foreigner."

The Critic stumbled past them to sit on a tree stump. He swabbed his forehead with his handkerchief. Now he recognized the little boy who had disturbed his dinner at the restaurant. What could Elza possibly want from this child? At least he was definitely not an ex-boyfriend. That would have been embarrassing, he decided. Elza continued examining Pisti and petting his head.

"I'm fine, restaurant lady," he said, squirming. "It was only a scratch. The doctor said it was nothing."

Elza pulled him to her chest.

"I'm sorry, Pisti," she said. "I'm so sorry."

"You're not angry at me?" he asked.

She shook her head.

The boy squirmed again and finally pulled himself away. He did not understand what she was going on about, or why she was so happy to see him, but once he realized he was not in danger, he felt pretty good. An adult had never apologized to him before, and it was an experience that made him feel different, important. He knew it was probably a good time to ask her for something. He had a feeling he wouldn't be refused.

"Hey, restaurant lady, I'm hungry. Buy me a hot dog!"

Elza laughed. She looked at the Critic, who was now wiping his neck with his handkerchief. She couldn't believe he was there. Sitting on a tree stump in her small city and looking like a sad bear. What was he doing here?

"Are you hungry?" she called out to him.

The Critic smiled. He felt confident, he felt as if anything were possible.

"Honestly, I'm a little peckish after all that pedaling," he answered. "I could stand an early dinner."

"I tell you what, Pisti," she said to the little boy. She was petting him again. She wouldn't let go of him. "Why don't we all go back to my restaurant, and I'll open it just for you. I'll show you the kitchen. You can look at the menu and pick whatever you like, and I'll make it for you. I will cook dinner just for you . . . or you can help me cook. Would you like that?"

Pisti liked this idea very much. He nodded vigorously. He had looked through that window on so many occasions and often wondered what it felt like to be a person sitting at the big oak tables and eating. He knew this was a good deal and a great opportunity. His head bobbed up and down and now he grabbed her hand. His fingers were sticky with cotton candy.

"Let's go right now," he said. "I have to be home at dark, or my uncles and aunties will be angry. It's all the way on the other side of town."

"Don't worry about that," Elza said. "We have plenty of time, and I will get you home. I would like to speak to them about you anyway."

"The fat man is coming too?" Pisti asked. He was still regarding the Critic warily.

"Yes," she said. "Do you mind?"

Pisti looked at the Critic, who was struggling to stand up. He laughed and shook his head.

"No. I don't mind," Pisti said. "He can come."

Elza turned to the Critic. "I have a pork loin in the refrigerator. Sound good?"

"Absolutely," he said. "Lead the way."

They left the forest and cut through the crowds. Not wanting to lose him again, Elza held onto Pisti's hand. For a while he squirmed, but soon he stopped, and then he clutched the Critic's hand as well. The three of them walked down the pebbled paths and Pisti kicked stones and plastic bottles. A few times, he even used the adults as a swing and kicked his legs into the air. He laughed loudly at his good fortune.

Broken flower stems and plastic cups littered the street and street cleaners were just beginning to collect them. Pisti let go a couple of times to look for change or cigarette butts, but he always returned to walk between them.

Elza and the Critic occasionally locked eyes over his little head.

They arrived at the deserted Centrum and turned the corner toward the restaurant. Pisti ran ahead and peeked through the window.

"Oh, you changed everything!" he called out. "It's so nice!"

Elza unlocked the door and held it open for them.

"Why don't you wash up for dinner and pick a seat?" she asked while walking to the kitchen. "Dinner will be ready soon."

"I want to help," Pisti said and ran ahead of her. "You said I could cook."

Acknowledgments

With sincerest affection, I would like to thank Zita, Benji, Mom, Dad, Sis, Jason, Eli, and Ezra.

I would also like to thank Christine Lawley, Betty Reed, John Peede, Laurel Snyder, Tony Grooms, Saul Adler, Frank Reiss, Tom Mullen, N. M. Kelby, Joseph Skibell, Rob Jenkins, and Jack Riggs. I'd like to thank the Ottos, Patricia Reimann, and Alexandra Pringle. I'd like to thank the fine students at Georgia State University, as well as the countless writers—published and unpublished—I've had the pleasure of working with for so many years. I also want to thank Kathy Belden, Rachel Mannheimer, and my agent, Bill Clegg!

Thank you all.

M. F.

Note on the Author

Marc Fitten was born in Brooklyn, USA and lived in Hungary from 1993–1998. He is the former editor of the *Chattahoochee Review* and of the Red Hen Press Literary Translation series. Marc Fitten's first novel, *Valeria's Last Stand*, was published in six countries. He lives in Atlanta.

www.marcfitten.com